MURDER IN UNSOUND MIND

ANNE CLEELAND

ARTEMIS
PRESS

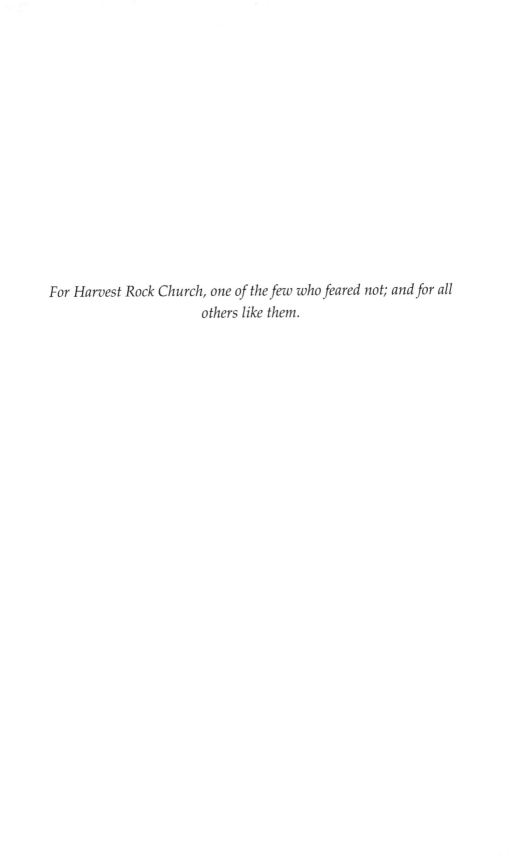

For Harvest Rock Church, one of the few who feared not; and for all others like them.

CHAPTER 1

Detective Sergeant Kathleen Doyle greeted the Police Constable who was guarding the perimeter outside the medical office building, and then ducked under the cordon-tape to hurry inside. DS Munoz had called her from the scene a half-hour ago, but Doyle hadn't got the message straightaway, because she'd been locked away, doing her exercises.

The building was an upscale one on Harley Street, and Doyle knew it well; it housed the medical offices of a good friend, and it had already featured as a crime scene in a recent homicide investigation—a doctor had been murdered, here. From what she'd gleaned from Munoz's message, however, it seemed unlikely this one was related to the first. You never knew, though, and best keep an open mind; Acton was always very skeptical when confronted with what seemed like a coincidence in a homicide case, and it did seem a bit strange that a posh building like this one would be hosting murderers, left and right.

As she walked down the interior hallway, she reached behind surreptitiously to draw her fingers along the bottom of her rucksack, hoping she'd remembered to bring along her electronics this morning—she hadn't known that a crime scene would be in the offing, and lately she tended to forget things—or forget things more than her usual, which was already a very low bar.

Good—she could feel the outline of her tablet; the last needful thing was to show up at sixes and sevens, what with Munoz watching her like a hawk.

"Nice of you to show up, Doyle."

Detective Sergeant Isabel Munoz had an edge to her tone, as she stood in the plush-carpeted hallway, and observed Doyle's approach. Munoz was a fellow Scotland Yard detective, and the two young women had a long history together, much of it not necessarily tranquil.

"Sorry," said Doyle. "Where's Tim?" Dr. Timothy McGonigal was her doctor-friend, and it was he who'd called-in the homicide when he'd come into his office this morning.

"He's downstairs—we're using the utility basement to hold the witnesses until we sort it out."

"What've we got?" Doyle asked, as she craned her neck around Munoz to see through the doorway.

"Female, mid-thirties. It may be a random; looks to be an unsound-mind."

Doyle made a face. "Yuck." An "unsound-mind" murder was exactly what it sounded like; the murderer had a wire crossed, and often the crime scene was a crackin' bloodbath, and not a sight for the faint of heart.

"This one's not too bad," Munoz said. "But it's a little weird."

"All right if I have a look?"

Doyle was forced to ask the question, because Munoz was the lead officer on site; she'd only called-in Doyle because she was aware that Doyle was friends with the reporting witness. There was also the off-chance that this case was indeed connected to the earlier murder, here in the building, and so Doyle should be included in the initial consult, so as to quickly verify whether the same team should be assigned—if the two cases were connected, the initial team would be miles ahead of any newly-assigned team in terms of solving the case.

"Look all you want, but you'll need to put on your gloves, first." There was a significant pause, whilst Munoz's eyes slid sidelong to meet hers.

Doyle could feel her face flush, and she retorted hotly, "I *know*, Munoz; this isn't my first homicide."

"Need any help?" the other girl asked, in a carefully neutral tone.

Struggling with what to say, Doyle finally replied in a stiff tone, "No, I don't." With a mighty effort, she managed to add, "Thank you."

Awkwardly, Doyle managed to pull on her gloves, acutely aware that Munoz was watching the process. In an abrupt tone, the other girl asked, "Does Acton know?"

Acton was Doyle's husband, a renowned Chief Inspector at the CID, and this reference only made Doyle's temper flare-up again. "That's *none* of your business, Izzy."

"Actually, it is."

The reminder was a sobering one; Doyle's wrist had been injured in a struggle with a suspect, and ever since, her left hand wasn't behaving itself properly. In particular, she was having trouble grasping objects, and since she was left-handed, this impairment tended to make day-to day tasks miles more difficult than they should have been.

Munoz had the right of it, and it was something they drilled into you at the Crime Academy; coppers tended to believe they could resolve their own problems—most notably, drugs or alcohol—but any impairment meant they were risking the lives of their fellow coppers. It was always best to get help, rather than try to tough it out alone.

In a constrained tone, Doyle offered, "It's gettin' better Munoz–truly. I'm doin' exercises, and I'd appreciate it if you didn't say anythin' to anyone." Reminded, she lifted her gaze to her companion in alarm. "Have you told Geary?" Munoz was herself married to a CID Inspector.

"No," the other said, and offered nothing more. "All right, then; let's have a look."

Doyle followed Munoz into the office suite's waiting room, and then paused in surprise on the threshold, as she beheld the murder victim on the floor. "Holy *Mother*."

In a dry tone, Munoz observed, "Seems a fairly clear case of unsound-mind."

Doyle could only agree; the victim was the young woman who'd acted as McGonigal's office manager, and Doyle was already familiar with her because she'd been an unwitting witness in the earlier homicide case. But this murder didn't seem to be connected to the first one, mainly because it was truly bizarre; the woman's arms were flung wide, with her wrists each nailed to the wooden floor, and a single entry-wound from a bullet squarely between her eyes. A computer print-out page had been left on her chest, containing the single word, "Harlot."

"A weird one," Munoz repeated. "There should be plenty of evidence, though."

This looked to be true; unsound-mind cases tended toward two ends of the spectrum; a crafty killer who hid his tracks—often a successful serial killer—or a deranged madman who didn't spare a thought about leaving buckets of evidence behind. This one would appear to fit the latter profile.

Doyle crouched to scrutinize the body, and blew out a resigned breath. "We should call-in Acton for a consult. He'd some dealings with this witness, in the earlier case."

"He's already been called-in; he's the Senior Investigating Officer."

Doyle nodded, and mentally crossed her fingers. It was early in the day, and so Acton should be sound enough for this case—it looked to be an easy one, after all, needing only the SOCO forensics team to come in and scoop up evidence a'plenty.

"It has religious overtures," Munoz observed as she crouched beside Doyle. "It almost resembles a crucifixion."

"Not to mention the 'harlot' tag, which seems more Biblical than not," Doyle agreed. "You're right; this looks to be an unsound-mind—it might be a 'random.'" This was actually a rarity; nine times out of ten, when a woman was murdered, it was by someone she knew well.

Munoz knit her brow. "There's plenty of security in this building, though. It's hard to see how a 'random' got through —she was murdered last night, judging by the state of the rigor, but the office closed at five."

Doyle frowned, as the two detectives silently thought this over for a moment. "Mayhap a security guard, or someone who would be on the premises late? It's unlikely that a medical patient would have stayed late, so as to do her in when no one else was here."

"But why would the victim stay late, instead of go home?" Munoz pointed out practically. "I think she was planning to meet someone, and it wasn't a 'random' after all."

But Doyle only made a skeptical sound. "She was stayin' after-hours to meet-up with an unsound-mind? I don't know as that's a decent workin'-theory, Munoz."

"The killer did call her a 'harlot'. Maybe he arranged for a hook-up, with the intent to kill her."

Doyle scoffed, "If he's that flashin'-lights crazy, Munoz, there's even less reason to think she'd have anythin' to do with him."

But Munoz was not about to relinquish her theory for the likes of Doyle, and insisted, "We should check to see if there are any psychiatry offices, in this building. A patient may have interacted with her—someone who seemed harmless, but who fixated on her as a target."

With a superior air, Doyle shook her head. "No—no psychiatrists in this buildin'; I already did a canvass with the first homicide. The psychiatrists tend to have offices down a few blocks." Doyle knew this for a fact, due to a best-be-forgot office visit that evolved into fisticuffs and a fat lip, once upon a time.

A knock on the doorjamb interrupted their mode-and-motive bickering, as the PC leaned in from the doorway. "DCI Acton is here, ma'am."

"Thank you," Munoz replied, as both girls rose.

Acton's tall figure appeared on the threshold, and Doyle's heart sank even as she mustered up a smile. He'd been drinking, even though it was only mid-morning. Not that he ever seemed to stop, nowadays—although he hid it well. Her husband was suffering from an acute case of remorse, being as the fair Doyle's latest altercation with a suspect could be laid squarely at his door. Acton had been squeezing his net a bit too tight, and the villains had panicked, hoping to create leverage by breaking into their flat, and attempting to seize hold of their small son. It hadn't worked—Doyle was not one to sit idly by, when it came to anyone's seizing Edward—and all was well that had ended well. Except for her hand, of course. And for the three villains; two had met a bad end, and one was awaiting manslaughter charges, courtesy of the Crown Court.

And except for her poor husband–whose own mental state tended to be a bit unsound at times, truth to tell. He was drowning in remorse and self-recrimination, and mainly doing it in the depths of a fine bottle of Scotch. Small chance that he hadn't noticed that her hand wasn't behaving itself properly—he was someone who noticed everything, especially when it came to his red-headed wife. But he'd made no mention, and so she'd made no mention, either, because all it needed was for Acton to feel even more remorseful than he already did—there wasn't enough scotch in the whole of London.

Hopefully, she'd set it all to rights soon; she'd consulted with a physiotherapist on the sly, who'd recommended exercises that were supposed to help her wrist. She was diligently visiting the place in secret, two times a week—no easy task, since Acton kept very close tabs on the wife of his bosom, even in ordinary circumstances.

Her rather disjointed thoughts were interrupted when Acton stepped into the room, his gaze resting on her for a moment before it swept over the corpse in an almost cursory fashion. "Good morning, Sergeant. What have we?"

"Good morning, sir," said Munoz, in her best lead-officer voice. "It's an odd one. Looks to be an unsound-mind."

Acton nodded, and looked over the scene for a moment in silence, his chin resting on his chest. "If you would call in the SOCOs, and alert the Coroner's office."

"Yes, sir. Shall I alert the other businesses in the area? If he's an unsound-mind, he may come back."

"Not as yet, I think."

Munoz stepped away to make her calls, and Acton took the opportunity to turn to Doyle, and run his hand along the length of her arm. It was a clear sign of his questionable state, because usually he avoided any public show of affection whilst they were on-duty. "Are you all right?" he asked gently.

"Right as rain," she pronounced with a bright, reassuring smile. The poor man wanted her well-away from here, being as he didn't much like it when his wedded wife was mucking about in grisly crime scenes. That, and he was worried about her, of course, and he allowed it to show, when he was in his cups.

To coax him out of the maudlins, she teased, "I am that tired of havin' to sort through your former light-o'-loves, Michael. You'd give that fellow—whatever his name was; the one with all his brides-in-the-bath—a run for his money."

He smiled slightly in grim acknowledgement, as he looked over her head to contemplate the victim. He'd been mildly flirtatious with this particular witness during the course of the old homicide case, so as to glean information from her. Acton was famous, titled and darkly handsome, and didn't hesitate to exploit this fortunate combination so as to gain an advantage with the fairer sex, whenever he felt it was needful.

Except for me, Doyle amended fairly. He never flirted with me for a single second, when we were first working together, which was just as well, since if he'd put it to the touch, I'd have probably run away to hide under the bed. A smart man, to assess the situation, and then proceed accordingly.

She'd first met her husband when she was assigned to be his support officer, until–one fine day–he'd proposed marriage, clear out of the blue. She'd readily accepted his offer; he was her commanding officer, after all—not to mention there was that darkly-handsome thing going on—and they'd been married straightaway, so that she didn't have any time to consider what it would be like to go from working-class Irish to an unlikely member of the British aristocracy. Not that she would have reconsidered, of course —she loved him fiercely, and he loved her even more than fiercely, if that was possible.

Indeed, it had come as a bit of a shock when she'd discovered, soon after they'd married, that Acton's take-no-prisoners courtship was part-and-parcel of his rather alarming overall philosophy; he was a vigilante, was Acton, and he wouldn't hesitate to manipulate evidence, or commit the occasional murder, himself, if he felt the justice system couldn't be trusted to come to the right result.

Thoroughly dismayed by this unsettling discovery—they were sworn to uphold the law, after all–Doyle tried to use her influence over him to convince him to mend his ways, with only mixed results, thus far. But being as she was the one person on earth who seemed to have any influence over him —not to mention that she loved the man—she persevered in what seemed like a rather daunting task, particularly when he was backsliding a bit, as he was now, all thanks to her stupid, *stupid* hand.

Still and all, there was nothing for it but to wait until he'd righted himself—and right himself he would, fingers crossed; they'd weathered a few of his black moods in the past, and he'd always managed to work through it. Best leave him to it; Acton was a complicated man–so complicated that even his cherished wife had barely scratched the surface—but there was no mistaking that they were good for each other, and that each of them was the better for having the other.

Not that anyone else had ever been given much of a chance to scratch his surface, of course; there was no denying the sad fact that more than a few of the women who'd made a run at Acton had wound up good and dead, for their sins.

Hard on this thought, Doyle suddenly stilled, and her reluctant gaze was drawn to the figure of the woman, fixed to the floor. Almost immediately, however, she decided that she was being fanciful; her husband's mind might be a teensy, tiny bit unsound, but not to the extent that he'd be murdering useful witnesses, and then labeling them as harlots, for good measure.

This rather troubling train of thought was interrupted when Acton suggested, "Perhaps if you would take a statement from McGonigal."

"Right." With a mental shake, she gathered-in her wayward thoughts. "Shall I release him, or will you need to speak with him after?"

"Release him," Acton decided. "Then text me, and I will drive you to headquarters."

This was somewhat of a surprise; usually Acton was like a hound-to-the-point, and frenetically busy when confronted with a new case—especially one like this, where it wasn't clear, as yet, whether they'd a rampaging unsound-mind on the loose. But before she could ask any follow-up questions, the SOCO team was announced, and he'd turned aside to issue instructions.

CHAPTER 2

*I*t's biting at me, Doyle acknowledged to herself. It's biting at me, and it shouldn't be.

She was seated in the utility basement, and she was supposed to be interviewing Dr. Timothy McGonigal, but her mind was wandering a bit, mainly because she was trying to decide why her intuition was acting up. Irish by birth, Doyle was what they would have called "fey" back home; she had a fine-tuned perceptive ability that allowed her to read the emotions of those in her immediate area, and—as a result of this—she could usually tell when someone was lying. It was a mixed blessing; it meant she didn't like venturing out in public, much, but it also meant she was a very useful detective, since homicide cases tended to feature lying liars who lied.

At present, she was trying to decide, with some misgiving, why she'd entertained such an unwelcome thought about Acton and the unfortunate victim upstairs.

There wasn't any connection, surely; he'd been semi-charming to the woman so as to glean some useful evidence —evidence that had led to the take-down of an illegal pharmaceuticals rig. And now that selfsame witness had been killed by some crazy kook with a grudge—

Doyle paused, and then released a breath that she hadn't realized she'd been holding. There was the nub of it, and it put paid to any uneasiness; the last thing Acton would do would be to perform a sensational murder like the one above-stairs; instead, an Acton-victim would simply disappear from sight, with no one the wiser.

Of course, there'd been a few exceptions to this rule, she reluctantly acknowledged, as she brought her attention back to the man seated before her—Tim McGonigal, who was currently expressing his surprise and deep dismay, as witnesses tended to do for the first few minutes of an interview. In fact, McGonigal's own sister was an exception to the Acton-rule, since her murder had been staged as a suicide. Still and all, the main point remained; a sensational kook-murder wasn't Acton's style, at all, and her own mind must be thoroughly unsound, to have even entertained such a thought for a single second.

Very much reassured, she re-focused her attention on the witness, and tried not to dwell on the unfortunate truth that her illustrious and well-respected husband had a recognizable murder-style. "Aye, Tim; 'tis indeed a terrible shock. Did the victim mention anyone who'd been botherin' her, lately? Old boyfriends, mayhap?"

McGonigal was a bluff, kindly man about Acton's age, and the two had gone to school together, back in the day. Indeed, it could be said that McGonigal counted as Acton's only friend, being as Acton wasn't exactly a friends-collecting type of person. Although neither was she, for that matter; instead, they were two solitary souls who'd stayed away from everyone else, yet somehow managed to find each other, thank God fastin'.

In response to her question, the doctor ducked his chin and looked a bit uncomfortable. "She was very—well, very 'modern', I guess you'd say. Seemed to like men."

"She definitely liked Acton," Doyle agreed with a small smile.

He met her eyes in rueful acknowledgment. "Yes; I wasn't going to say, but she did ask after him—asked if I knew his contact information—and I had to remind her to please be professional." He lowered his voice. "Not that she'd listen, I'm afraid; I'm fairly certain she was having an affair with Dr. Benardi, before he was killed."

"That's all very interestin', Tim, but Dr. Benardi's not a potential suspect," Doyle reminded him. Dr. Benardi's death was the previous homicide that they'd investigated, here. "Was there anyone more recently? Or did it seem to you that anyone was pesterin' her?"

He furrowed his brow. "I don't think anyone was pestering her—or at least, not that she mentioned. She'd an Italian boyfriend who seemed very keen, but I haven't seen him for months."

Doyle nodded, resigned. It was too much to hope for, that the woman had been fighting with an identifiable lover–one who could then be easily identified on the CCTV cameras that were street-level, so that they could roll him up before lunch.

"I have to say–it doesn't seem like a lover's crime, to me,"

McGonigal added in a doubtful tone. "It seems too–too cold and calculating, I suppose; to desecrate a corpse, and then leave a sign, the way he did."

There was a small pause, whilst Doyle frowned, trying to decide what was meant. "I didn't notice that the corpse was desecrated, Tim," she ventured. She and Munoz had taken a careful look, after all, and they'd seen no such signs.

Turning a bit pink, McGonigal hurriedly explained, "Oh—oh, I meant the nails in the hands, Kathleen. It was done post-mortem."

"Aye; of course, it was," Doyle agreed slowly, as she pictured the scene in her mind. "There wasn't any blood." Wounds inflicted post-mortem didn't bleed, since the victim's heart had already stopped beating. So that meant that this killer—this killer hadn't sought to terrorize his victim; instead, he'd decided to nail her hands to the floor after she was already dead. Which seemed a bit pointless, even for an unsound-mind.

Thinking on this, Doyle asked, "Is there a printer, in that room?"

Her companion spread his hands. "No—there's very little need for one, anymore. We all share a printer here in the basement, on those rare occasions where there's a patient who doesn't have the tech to receive documents electronically."

"So," she mused, "he must have brought along his hammer, and his nails, and his harlot-sign, which means it's very unlikely he'll get off with an unsound-mind defense."

McGonigal raised his brows in surprise. "Oh? I would think it apparent."

But Doyle shook her head. "Not in criminal law, Tim.

Faith, if you started talkin' about degrees of craziness in murder, it turns into a crackin' tangle-patch, because most normal people would agree that *any* murder involves a degree of craziness, to begin with. Not to mention that crooks are clever—as are their counsel—and so it would be a relatively simple thing to feign an unsound-mind so as to avoid prison, and instead be sent to some institution for a dose of tender lovin' care."

"Oh," her companion replied, as he thought this through. "I see."

Doyle nodded in affirmation. "Instead, they draw the defense very narrowly. The test is whether your mind is so unsound that you're not even aware what you're doin' is wrong. If this fellow brought along his tools beforehand to do the job, it would put a nail in any unsound-mind defense."

With a sad sigh, McGonigal added, "And he must have arranged to meet with her—it does seem as though she was waiting, after-hours. He must have been very determined; I do hope you catch him."

But Doyle had handled a fair number of homicides, and so could reassure him, "Whist; not to worry, Tim. This killer's a bold one, and oftentimes the bold ones trip themselves up by their very boldness. I have high hopes we'll catch somethin' on the CCTV tape from the street outside—although the city's not always up-to-speed on camera maintenance, and shame on them."

Indeed, Doyle had worked a recent case at a free medical clinic, where the CCTV cameras had been purposefully disabled by the villains. And—come to think of it—that selfsame recent case had touched on Dr. Benardi's murder—the doctor who'd been killed here, previously. A small world, it was.

Doyle's scalp prickled, as it did when her intuition was telling her that it wasn't such a small world at all, and that it might behoove the fair Doyle to pay closer attention.

Trying to decide what had caught her attention, she ventured, "Tell me, Tim; did your office manager have any connection to the free clinic? Did she volunteer there, alongside you and Dr. Benardi?"

With a small shake of his head, McGonigal replied, "No. I'm afraid she was not one to volunteer. And certainly no one wants to volunteer now, after so many murders. I think the staff has all quit, and we may have to close our operating suite." In deep sorrow, he shook his head. "Such a terrible shame."

But Doyle was frowning in puzzlement. "How many murders were there? More than Dr. Benardi, and Dr. James?"

He glanced up. "Oh—oh; the other one's not really connected to the illegal pharmaceuticals problem, Kathleen. Instead, it was just a spot of terrible luck, and so very untimely. We were making an effort to get the patients to come back to the clinic, after all the unpleasantness was settled, and so the staff was going door to door, passing out pamphlets—I knocked on a few doors, myself. Unfortunately, the charge-nurse knocked on the wrong door, and was killed by a deranged transient." McGonigal lowered his voice. "Horrible; the fellow skewered him with a sword."

Doyle blinked in astonishment. "The clinic's charge-nurse was *murdered*?" This was very unexpected; the last Doyle had heard, the man was a cooperating witness in the illegal pharmaceuticals case.

"Oh–I thought you knew, Kathleen."

"No—it isn't my homicide case," she explained a bit

absently. "And if it's not connected to the clinic case, I wouldn't necessarily hear about it."

As she tried to process this unlooked-for turn of events, she thought in surprise, why—there's something here; something I should pay attention to. Between the charge-nurse and Tim's office manager, two helpful witnesses from the illegal pharmaceuticals case have been murdered, even though it seemed as though the mode and manner were completely different, for each of the two murders—

"Oh—oh, right. I tend to assume that you and Acton always together work as a team, and I forget that's not the case at all."

With an effort, she brought her attention back to her witness. "No—Acton has a lot of oversight responsibility, over a ton of other cases, and I don't always hear the latest. In fact, he doesn't much like to talk shop at home—not unless I winkle it out of him; he's the next thing to a sphynx."

With an attempt at off-handedness, her companion ventured, "How's he doing? Acton, I mean."

For a brief moment, Doyle struggled with how to reply, since it seemed clear that McGonigal was aware that Acton was currently off his pins. In all honesty, she said, "You never truly know, do you?"

Immediately, the doctor leaned forward to apologize. "Forgive me, Kathleen; I intrude."

Doyle mustered up a small smile. "Faith, Tim; that's what friends are for, and if anyone's entitled to intrude, it's you."

Clearly uncomfortable, her companion quickly moved on to another subject. "Then I will further intrude, and ask how you are feeling, Kathleen—you're starting to bloom, a bit."

These waters were not as deep, since Doyle was a few

months pregnant with their second child. "I'm goin' grand, Tim," she replied, and wished that this was true.

"I am happy to hear it," he said a bit wistfully. "You are so lucky, the two of you."

Aware that poor McGonigal was not exactly what you'd call lucky in love, Doyle joked, "We will see–it's goin' to be a three-ring circus, my friend, and I'll expect you to jump in with both feet."

"Of course," he promised with a smile. "Is Mary on maternity leave, as yet?"

Mary was Doyle's nanny, who was expecting her own baby in the near future. McGonigal himself had once been keen on sweet, gentle Mary—faith, who hadn't been? But the woman had married an up-and-coming politician, and—as always seemed the case—McGonigal had been a step too slow.

It's so unfair, Doyle thought; he's such a kind man, but he never seems interested in the type of woman who'd match him—someone just as kind, who'd jump at the chance to be a prominent surgeon's wife.

In response to his question, she replied, "Mary's not on maternity leave as yet, but we're prepared; Acton's enlisted a girl from Trestles to help her out for now, and then substitute for Mary during her leave." Trestles was Acton's hereditary estate, and tended to be chock-full of people who'd fall on their sword for the House of Acton. It was a strange and foreign concept to someone like Doyle, who thought any emphasis on bloodlines was ridiculously outdated, and ran counter to the basic tenets of her religious beliefs. But she'd seen its power in action too many times to doubt it—where people would look to Acton for leadership without hesitation, and sometimes against their better judgment.

Indeed, it was one of the reasons Acton got away with the things he got away with; he wielded extraordinary power, all thanks to an ancient title that was probably bestowed upon one of his ancestors for some very questionable behavior in the first place.

Doyle brought her wandering thoughts back to the topic at hand, and continued, "I'm sorry to say that I doubt Mary will be comin' back–what with her own family to tend to–but life moves on, and so now we have a new nanny, learnin' the ropes. She'll need your prayers, because our Edward is a handful."

McGonigal joked a bit sadly, "Well, ask Acton if there's anyone at Trestles who'd can step in as my office manager— I'll be needing a new one."

Doyle shook her head in sympathy. "I'm that sorry you've had such a mornin', my friend. Here's to better days."

"Amen," he replied. "What happens now?"

"The SOCOs should be here for a couple of hours, and then I imagine you will be cleared to go back in. I'll have a DC go over your statement, so that you can affirm it before you leave—it shouldn't take long."

Her companion nodded. "There's no rush–I've cleared my schedule, and I should contact that poor young woman's family. It's always a difficult task—to try to comfort the family when surgery doesn't go well—and I imagine this will be much the same."

Doyle nodded, and—with a stoic attitude—prepared to handle her own difficult task by texting Acton to let him know she was finishing up with Tim.

Nothin' for it, she thought, as her mobile pinged in response; I've got to face the wretched music, and have it out with the man. It's no easy thing for either one of us; he's in fortress-Acton, and in my own way, I'm in fortress-Doyle, and neither of us wants to set foot outside. But if McGonigal's noticed that Acton is drinking too much, he won't be the last, and I've got to stop being such a baby, and straighten the man out. As my mother used to say, in for a penny, in for a pound.

Mentally girding her loins, she walked outside to wait for her husband at the perimeter.

CHAPTER 3

*O*n his way out of the building, Acton ran into the coroner's assistant who was on his way in, and so he stopped to confer with the man for a few minutes whilst Doyle waited at the foot of the steps.

He does look a bit drawn, she thought with a pang; I haven't been paying attention—being as I've too been busy visiting physiotherapists, and trying not to use my hand in his presence. Shame on me; Tim is showing more concern about the man than I am, and that won't do a'tall.

Acton concluded his conversation, and approached her, his eyes meeting hers. "Anything?"

"Not a blessed thing, which only makes sense, because I imagine Tim steered well-away from having any knowledge about the victim's personal life. He thought she was havin' an affair with Dr. Benardi—which only goes with the territory, I suppose—and he also mentioned that she'd an Italian boyfriend, some months past. No indication that an unsound-mind has been stalkin' her, lately."

He nodded, and steered her in the direction where his Range Rover was parked. It was cold, and so she hunched her shoulders as they walked a few steps in silence. "Want me to drive?" she offered.

There was a small, significant pause. "Is it that evident?" he asked quietly.

"Only to me, my friend."

"I am capable," he said, as he opened the door for her. "I am sorry, Kathleen."

She made a wry mouth, as she slid into the seat. "You'll be sorrier still, Michael, because drunk or sober, we're goin' to have a discussion, and I'm afraid there's no bunkin' it." Her tone was necessarily firm, because Acton tended to avoid any and all personal discussions. Small blame to the man, when you thought about it; his still waters ran very, very deep.

But this seemed to be the one occasion where he wasn't as reluctant as was his usual, because once he closed the door behind him, he turned to face her, instead of engaging the engine. "Tell me what I should do," he said quietly, his gaze fixed upon hers, "and I will do it."

She caught a glimpse of his distress, before it was quickly muffled; Acton knew all about her perceptive abilities, and he was one of the few people that she couldn't easily read—no doubt because he didn't wish her to, and he'd an iron control over his emotions. Or usually he did, that was, which meant that the poor man was sunk in such misery that he was having trouble disguising it.

Thoroughly dismayed that he was so very unhappy—it only went to show that she'd been handling this all wrong; *of course* he was blaming himself, and *of course* her attempt to pretend that nothing was amiss only made everything miles worse—she took a breath, and admitted, "There's naught for you to do, Michael—it's just takin' a bit longer than I thought it would. I'm sorry I didn't let you know; shame on me."

He didn't move, and she didn't move, and she felt a bit sorry for the both of them. In a strange way, it reminded her of his proposal of marriage, when they'd been sitting in a car in much the same way, each locked away in their respective fortresses.

"Can you tell me of your symptoms? I'd like to have a better understanding, if I may."

She could feel herself flush, and found that she had trouble meeting his eyes—she was that ashamed. "My hand wasn't behavin' itself properly—goin' numb and tinglin', from time to time—more of an annoyance, than anythin' else. So, I tried to hide it, which I shouldn't have, and let this be a lesson." She lifted her face to say with all sincerity, "I've been doin' exercises, and they seem to be helpin'."

Gently, he took up her hands in his own. "Good. I am glad to hear of it."

Encouraged by his reaction—milder than what she'd been expecting, all in all—she continued, "I've been seein' a physiotherapist for two visits a week, but I truly don't know as I'll need many more, since I can do the exercises all on my own, now." She paused, and then added in a rush, "I'm so, so sorry I was sneakin' about without tellin' you, Michael; please tell me that you forgive me."

Bending his head, he contemplated her hands in his for a moment. "The fault is mine. You felt you could not tell me."

"Well, that, and the therapist is a handsome man," she teased.

He smiled slightly in response, but it took an effort, and so she immediately lifted one of his hands, so as to kiss its back.

"Forgive me, Michael, and let this be a lesson not to try to work things out on my own, with secret plans, and such."

But—as always—in Acton's eyes, she could do no wrong. "You only did so because you felt you could not tell me."

In mild exasperation, she observed, "We're goin' 'round and 'round, husband, and we'll be here till dinnertime." Suddenly struck, she added, "Think on it; I couldn't be honest, because I was afraid that you'd be sunk in remorse, but you were already sunk in remorse because I wasn't being honest with you. It's like that story—the one where the husband and wife were each sacrificin' for the other, but it turned out it was at cross-purposes."

"*The Gift of the Magi.*"

She shook her head impatiently. "No, no; the story's not about *Christmas*, Michael. I'll think of it, don't worry."

He gently squeezed the hands in his. "I am truly sorry, Kathleen."

She mustered up a reassuring smile. "There's nothin' to be sorry about, husband. I'm havin' a weak spell, and you're havin' a weak spell because I'm havin' a weak spell, and 'round and 'round it goes, which is what's bound to happen when you've two people who'd rather be flayed alive than have a heart-to-heart discussion."

He smiled in return—a genuine smile, which was encouraging. "There is that."

Thinking to build upon his lighter mood, she wheedled, "Is there any chance you can drop whatever you're doin', so that we can go home for a bit? We could have lunch with Edward, and then you could have a lie-down, mayhap." Mainly, she wanted to make certain that no one else would be given the chance to entertain the extraordinary notion that the illustrious Chief Inspector had been drinking like an alderman before noon.

But he shook his head slightly, and relinquished her hands with regret. "As tempting as that sounds, I am afraid I cannot, just now. I must contact Sir Vikili, and arrange for a surrender into custody."

She raised her brows, because this was of interest; Sir Vikili was a famous criminal-defense solicitor, wily and well-known for getting his questionable clients off the hook. He and Acton were often on opposite sides of high-profile homicide cases, and the man would not be happy with the idea of having to surrender one of his well-heeled clients into Detention—no doubt he'd feel it was beneath him.

"Now, there's a come-uppance," she remarked. "What's the case?"

"This one," he replied, as he turned to start-up the car.

She blinked in surprise. "Faith, Michael; you've sussed-out the perp, already? Now, there's some good detectin', and my hat's off to you. So; the killer is one of Sir Vikili's clients?"

This would be quite the surprise, actually; Sir Vikili tended to represent high-level criminals, engaged in high-level criminal enterprises, being as his services were ridiculously expensive. So, this was unlooked-for—that one of his clients was an unsound-mind—but it just went to show that you never knew.

Her husband checked the mirror briefly, before he pulled into traffic. "I have the advantage of knowing that Antonio D'Angelo had an affair with the victim."

Doyle stared at him, open-mouthed—Mother a' *Mercy*, but Munoz's morning assignment was brimful of massive surprises. Antonio D'Angelo was now dead, but his wife was very much alive, and under indictment for voluntary manslaughter–said manslaughter having occurred when she'd killed her husband during the donnybrook at Doyle's flat.

Martina was currently out on her own recognizance, because—even though she'd killed her husband—she'd been charged with manslaughter instead of murder, due to the circumstances surrounding the homicide. That, and also due to the happy fact that she'd hired Sir Vikili as her defense solicitor, and the man made a fine living pulling people's coals out of the fire.

"Holy *Mother*," she breathed in abject wonder; "You think it was *Martina*, who killed this office manager?"

"It does seem evident."

This was true; Martina Betancourt was consumed with all the fervor of a religious zealot, and she'd killed her own husband out of a righteous sense of heavenly justice. It appeared she wasn't about to allow this particular harlot– who'd led her husband astray—to wiggle off the vengeance- hook, and so said harlot had been made to pay a terrible price. Indeed, they already knew that Martina had killed another one of Antonio's girlfriends, and so it all made complete sense—not to mention that this must be why Doyle's instinct had been prodding her this morning; prodding her about a connection to the other murders at the free clinic. This murder was indeed related to those, only not in the usual way; it was a retribution murder, pure and simple.

Doyle closed her eyes because this seemed important, for some reason, but she couldn't seem to catch hold of the thought. Slowly, she reasoned, "Then mayhap we should do an exigent search for any others—other Antonio-girlfriends.

Otherwise, Martina may lay waste to half of London, when all is said and done."

Acton glanced over at her as he drove. "Not after today; she'll be in custody."

"Oh—oh, that's right. And not a moment to soon," Doyle agreed rather absently, because her scalp had started prickling again.

CHAPTER 4

*O*nce back at headquarters, Doyle parted ways with Acton at the lobby's lifts—his office was up amongst the brass, whilst her cubicle was down amongst the bottom-feeders–and she was not at all surprised to receive a visit from Munoz even before she'd settled into her desk.

The Spanish girl's dark eyes were alight with excitement, as she leaned on Doyle's cubicle wall. "Did you hear?"

"I did indeed," Doyle replied as she lowered her rucksack to the floor with her off-hand. "Are you going over to Bookin', to watch the show?"

Munoz shook her head. "No, Acton wanted to handle it, and I'd just be in the way of the alpha-lions."

Doyle had to smile at this characterization—watching Acton battle with Sir Vikili was a sight to behold; rather like watching a knife-fight break out in the House of Lords. "Well, you're an alpha-lioness, if that's any consolation."

"It is, as a matter of fact, and I appreciate the thought. Did Williams get hold of you?"

Detective Inspector Thomas Williams was Doyle's good friend, and they often worked assignments together. "Not as yet. What's up?"

The other girl shrugged. "I don't know—he was here looking for you, early this morning."

No more sneaking away for therapy, Doyle thought; mental note. "I'll ping him, then. Who's writin' up the report for this mornin's investigation, you or me?"

"I am," Munoz said. "Acton asked me to, and he'd rather your role was reduced."

With a frustrated breath, Doyle blew a tendril of hair off her forehead. "He knows about my hand, and so he wants to wrap me in cotton-wool, the knocker. But I can type fine–I just can't hold things, very well."

"Like a gun?"

Very much on her dignity, Doyle replied, "Why, what a strange thing to say, Munoz; I am not sanctioned to carry a gun."

But Munoz only shrugged. "Geary wants me to carry one, too."

This was of interest; Munoz had recently married a Detective Inspector—an Irishman, on loan from Dublin's *Garda*—and he'd apparently decided to overlook the strict gun protocols, when it came to his new wife's safety. And it was probably not a coincidence that Inspector Geary felt emboldened to do so, being as the man had recently discovered that Acton's wife also carried an illegal gun.

"It's come in handy," Doyle admitted. "And on more than one occasion."

Her injured hand started tingling at this reminder of the last, memorable occasion when she'd fired her gun, and so Doyle tucked it under her other arm, so as to still it. She added, "I told Acton we should have a look at all the unsolved homicides in the past month or so, to see if Martina Betancourt has killed any of Antonio's other girlfriends."

Munoz was checking the messages on her mobile, and she replied absently, "You'd think it would be a lot simpler just to kill him and be done with it, rather than go after all the girlfriends."

"Spoken like a true newlywed, Munoz."

But Munoz paused in her message-reading to look up. "It's true," she insisted. "It sounds like a case of projection to me. She's furious with him, but it's much easier to blame the other women than it is to blame her cheating husband."

Doyle considered this, but then pointed out, "She did wind up killin' him, Munoz, even though she loved the man. It's a sad case of thwarted-love, all dressed-up as righteousness."

Munoz made a derisive sound, and went back to checking her messages. "Shooting your husband, for his own good? There's an unsound-mind, if I ever heard one."

Doyle could only concede this point. "Aye; I think most people would likely agree with you, and I think that was the theory Sir Vikili was usin' to lay the groundwork for a voluntary manslaughter charge—she may not get off with an unsound-mind defense, but she should nonetheless get somethin' less than murder-one. Of course, now that she's haled off and killed one of Antonio's girlfriends in the meantime, her goose is well-and-thoroughly cooked, and she's lookin' at murder-one with no mitigatin' circumstances."

Munoz raised her brows. "You don't think Sir Vikili will try to bring an unsound-mind defense? This one looks crazier than the murder of the husband—she's only getting worse."

But Doyle only shook her head, having already gone over this ground with McGonigal. "No—not if she brought-in the tools, and the 'harlot' sign. She knew what she was doin', and so an 'unsound-mind' defense is off the table. She'll get twenty years in a Class A prison, if she gets a day."

Munoz shut her eyes, briefly. "Ugh. If I had that to look forward to, it would be time to climb into the tub, and slit my wrists."

"She doesn't dare, Munoz; suicide is a mortal sin."

"Good point. Then maybe she can join-up with the Prison Ministry, while she's doing hard time."

With a touch of skepticism, Doyle replied, "I doubt they'd take her, Munoz. They're all evangelicals, in Prison Ministry, and Martina's a hard-line RC—faith; harder-line than most."

But the other girl only pointed out, "They'll take anyone— that's the whole point of Prison Ministry."

Doyle refrained from pointing out in turn that a hard-line RC may not choose to congregate with evangelicals in the first place, and instead conceded, "I suppose you've the right of it. And speakin' of takin'-in just anyone, how was Dublin?" Munoz had recently returned from a trip to meet her new in-laws.

The other girl paused to look up, and smile at the memory. "It was a freak-show. Everyone sounds just like you."

Doyle chuckled. "Now you know how I feel, Munoz. Were they civil, at least?"

"Very. I met all the relatives—a huge herd of them—and they're happy he's happy. I feel as though I've won the lottery, even though I wasn't even playing."

"Now I'm hearin' a true newlywed," Doyle teased.

But Munoz only countered, "Don't try to say you didn't

win the lottery with Acton, because no one would believe you."

Doyle shrugged. "No one's perfect, Munoz." Understatement of the century, right there. "I suppose it always takes some gettin' used to—pullin' a double harness."

"It's easier when you have a lot in common," Munoz offered. "Geary comes from a long line of coppers."

"Coppers tend to run in families, Munoz. You and I are the exception."

The other girl lifted a brow. "Along with Williams, and Acton, and Gabriel."

"Oh—I guess our little group is the exception, then." Doyle hesitated, but then decided that she may as well ask. "How is Gabriel, by-the-by?" Officer Gabriel had been Munoz's beau until he was rather abruptly supplanted by Munoz's new husband.

Munoz made a face. "Geary doesn't want me to socialize with him, which is a little awkward. He thinks Gabriel still carries a torch."

With a sympathetic sound, Doyle offered, "And there's thwarted-love, rearing its ugly head, again. It's almost a shame that everyone can't wind up with who they long for, but that's not the way it works."

"We're lucky, I guess."

"Indeed, we are," Doyle agreed, and decided to say no more on the subject. Her mobile pinged, and she glanced at the screen. "There's Williams, so I'm off."

Immediately, Munoz's brows drew together. "He'd better not be giving you all the good assignments."

Doyle soothed, "Not to worry, Munoz; no one would ever mistake me for an alpha-lioness."

"You're the one with the commendations," the other girl

reminded her in a pointed manner. Doyle had been awarded two separate commendations for bravery under best-be-forgot circumstances, one of which had heavily featured the fair Munoz.

With a conciliatory smile, Doyle replied, "You forget that I'm disabled, now, so I'll not be on the receivin' end of any commendations. Instead I'm reduced to havin' you write-up my reports."

"Get un-disabled then," the other advised in an annoyed tone. "I've better things to do."

CHAPTER 5

homas Williams was a Detective Inspector, which meant that he out-ranked Doyle and was another one who inhabited the exalted upper floors of management. She couldn't resent this fact, because Williams was a very good detective with an excellent track-record. That, and Williams was always Acton's first choice as a Crime Scene Manager, which meant that everyone else in the CID brass tended to approve of Williams, so as to follow suit.

It's that bloodline thing again—like that emperor who was wearing no clothes, Doyle thought; Acton's highly respected, and no one would dare question his judgment, even though many of his judgments couldn't withstand the light of day. He knows it, of course, and wields it ruthlessly; faith, I've seen this particular superpower in action too many times to question its might, even if I may question its value.

This rather ambivalent train of thought came to an end when Doyle appeared in William's doorway, and he looked up from his desk to signal her in. Williams had been

Doyle's good friend through thick and thin, starting back from their days together at the Crime Academy. After she'd married Acton, however, she'd soon realized that the reason Acton favored Williams so much was because the two men shared the same alarming philosophy—that the justice system needed a push, now and again, to get to the correct result, and neither man would hesitate to administer that push.

Since Doyle was of the opinion that the justice system shouldn't be hijacked by anyone–no matter how well-meaning–this led to the occasional divided-loyalties situation, where Doyle would try to prevail upon Williams to help pull Acton back from the brink, with Williams not always eager to do so. Despite this, they'd settled into a warm friendship, and Doyle counted Williams as a staunch friend.

Williams closed his laptop. "Shut the door, will you?"

Doyle hesitated. "Can we go get a coffee, instead? I should try and avoid any closed-door meetings with handsome men, for the foreseeable future."

With some surprise, he rose and shrugged into his suit jacket. "What's happened?"

But Doyle had belatedly come to the realization that mayhap she shouldn't keep blurting things out—mental note —and so she hedged, "You go first."

"Let's get outside, first."

This was of interest, in that it appeared Williams didn't want to be overheard telling her whatever it was he wanted to tell her as they walked through the building—the hallways and lifts were under constant surveillance, and so it was always the better part of discretion to have private conversations off-campus. Therefore, as they walked down the hallway toward the lift, Doyle spoke of the first random thought that entered her mind. "Who d'you think would win, in a knife-fight between Munoz and Lizzy?"

Lizzy was Lizzy Mathis, who worked in the forensics lab, and was another of Acton's henchmen—or a henchwoman, more properly. The young woman had found herself married to Williams rather unexpectedly, and—as far as Doyle knew —it was not at all clear whether the two had decided to go forward with the marriage, or to part amicably with an annulment. Doyle asked the question because—despite his erstwhile wife's rather dry demeanor—Lizzy Mathis was just as formidable as Munoz, in her own way.

Williams smiled slightly as they stepped into the lift. "Are they really going to have a knife-fight? I should sell tickets."

Doyle laughed. "I was just talkin' with Munoz about how she's an alpha-lioness, but I think Lizzy's an alpha-lioness in her own right, and so I'm not at all certain who'd come out the winner."

"Lizzy," her companion decided, as the doors slid open and they stepped within. "Munoz has gone soft."

"Well, she's a newlywed, Thomas. Just like you." With a significant pause, Doyle slid her gaze over to him as they descended to the lobby. Williams never referred to his marriage, and never, ever referred to Lizzy as his "wife," so she thought she'd dare to needle him a bit.

But Williams was Williams, and was not about to give her any insights into his personal life. "I'm not sure that I could best either one of them with an edged-weapon," he admitted. "And with that in mind, I'd better behave myself."

"Well, Munoz is worried you're wantin' to give me a good assignment instead of her, so I may be the one who falls victim to her blade."

He tilted his head, as they exited the lift into the lobby.

"What's she complaining about? She had a new homicide this morning, didn't she?"

"She did indeed, but it was an open-and-shut case, as it turned out."

They walked across the spacious lobby, the busy area echoing with murmured voices. "Really? What happened?"

Again, Doyle was suddenly aware that she was gabbling without a thought to her audience, and a pox on her wretched, wretched tongue. Although to be fair, Williams was going to find out, sooner or later, and so she may as well get over this crackin' minefield as quickly as possible. "Acton thinks Martina Betancourt killed the victim in a fit of jealous rage."

Because he was the opposite of a gabbler, Williams managed to contain his response until they were well-outside the building, and then he turned to her with all incredulity. "*Martina?*"

His surprise was understandable; Williams had dated Martina for a time—without being aware that the woman was married–and therefore he'd been a bit crushed, poor man, when he'd discovered this inconvenient little fact. To the good, he certainly seemed to have recovered quite nicely, ever since his own strange and unexpected marriage.

Doyle nodded. "Aye, Acton's arrangin' with Sir Vikili for a surrender-into-custody even as we speak. It turns out that the victim had an affair with Martina's husband, and—since Martina's the bloody-vengeance type—this didn't sit well."

"Wow," her companion exclaimed, thoroughly surprised.

"Wow, indeed. And speakin' of such, when it comes to knife-fights, I'd put my money on Martina against all comers, thank you very much."

Still coming to grips with the revelation, Williams could

only shake his head in wonder. "Sir Vikili would probably like to kill her, himself. He was greasing the skids for a voluntary manslaughter charge, and now that's completely out the window."

Doyle could only agree. "Can you imagine his frustration? Those pesky clients; halin' off and murderin' people, just when you were about to get 'em off the hook."

He blew out a breath. "She's looking at hard time."

"Hard time in a hard place, like Maghaberry," Doyle agreed, referring to the notorious prison in the north of Ireland.

He glanced down at her. "Unlikely she'd go there, Kath; that's for men."

"Oh, right." They walked a few steps in silence, until she observed, "I know Martina's not an 'unsound-mind,' since the murder was clearly planned out ahead of time, but truly, she *does* have an unsound-mind, and I feel a bit sorry for her. She loved her husband to distraction, and it's addled her brain."

"I suppose."

She could see that he was troubled about it, and small blame to him; he'd been very keen on Martina, once upon a time, and that time was actually not very long ago. She squeezed his arm, and offered, "You dodged a bullet, my friend."

He lifted his brows, and replied fairly, "Only so long as Lizzy isn't plotting to murder me."

"Now, there's a fair point," she agreed, with a show of solemnity. "It may be a case of the fry-pan and the fire."

"Tell me what's happened with Acton, and secret meetings with men."

A bit flustered, Doyle reminded him, "You were supposed to go first."

"First, I'd like to make sure Acton's not going to be fighting Lizzy for the pleasure of knifing me."

She blew out an exasperated breath. "No, Thomas—it wasn't that type of secret meetin', and I shouldn't have implied that it was. Instead, it was stupid. Or, more properly, I was stupid, and I handled it all wrong, and so I had to beg his pardon fastin'."

He glanced down at her as he held open the Deli's door. "Handled what?"

She shrugged, as they made their way through the tables toward the counter. "My stupid hand."

"What about your hand?"

She explained over her shoulder, "I hurt it, and it's not working properly."

He lifted his brows in surprise. "Is that so? I hadn't noticed."

CHAPTER 6

*T*hey bought a quick cup of coffee—technically, Doyle was not supposed to be drinking coffee whilst pregnant, but every now and again she slipped the leash and took a mouthful or two—no harm done, surely, and hopefully she hadn't contributed to the undeniable fact that her first-born was a rolling ball of energy.

After they'd settled in to a table, she savored her first sip before asking him, "So; what's the thing you're wantin' to tell me?

With the air of someone disclosing an interesting bit of news, he met her eyes as he leaned back in his chair. "You'll never guess who called me, yesterday."

"The Pope," Doyle guessed promptly.

He smiled. "Even more unexpected than the Pope."

"Who?"

"Philippe Savoie."

Doyle stared, and slowly lowered her coffee cup. "Savoie? Called *you*? Whatever for?"

"Thankfully, not a knife-fight."

"Amen to that," Doyle agreed. Philippe Savoie was an international criminal, with an occurrence sheet as long as your arm. The Frenchman had managed to stay one step ahead of his own lengthy prison term, mainly because he was very shrewd, but also because he and Doyle were friends-of-sorts, starting from the time he'd saved the fair Doyle's life on a best-be-forgot occasion. This meant that Doyle's husband—who was supposedly sworn to help prosecute blacklegs like Savoie—instead felt that he owed the man a debt of honor, which in turn protected Savoie from any legal come-uppance for his crimes. That, and he was another on the long list of questionable people represented by the great and mighty Sir Vikili.

But all this notwithstanding, it was passing strange that the Savoie would contact Williams, of all people. Savoie and Williams had a history of not liking each other much–not very much at all–to the point where each would have gladly knocked the other down and called it a good day's work.

Williams' expression grew more serious. "I suppose you could say that he gave me a tip, in a manner of speaking. It's something of a delicate situation, which is why he felt he couldn't call you. He was concerned enough to follow-up, though, and decided to call me, instead."

Thoroughly intrigued by this preamble, Doyle prompted, "Unsnabble, Thomas; whatever did he say?"

"He said that he was at the park yesterday afternoon, and that Mary was there with Edward."

Doyle nodded, as this was nothing unusual; Mary-the-nanny often took Doyle's son to the park across the street from their residential building, so as to expend some of the toddler's considerable energy. And–being as the playground was a short walk from the school Savoie's son's attended–Savoie often met them there after school was out, so that Emile could play with Mary's own daughter, and with little Edward.

Although he hailed from France, Savoie had decided to live in London, for a time, so as to send his young son to a posh primary school, close by to where Doyle lived. It was a bit unexpected, all in all; Savoie had sailed very close to the wind, in recent events, and Doyle had assumed he would go home to lie low in France, for the nonce. He hadn't, however, and—as Doyle was aware that the Frenchman tended to collaborate with her husband on some rather questionable activities—she felt it behooved her not to ask too many questions about his decision to live in London, and so she didn't.

"Savoie called to inform me that Mary had a—well, I guess you'd call it a level-one altercation with Lady Abby."

This was unwelcome news, and Doyle slowly lowered her coffee cup. "Mother a' Mercy, Thomas; Lady Abby's here, in London? What happened?"

"Savoie told me that Lady Abby approached Mary, and wanted to speak with her—pestered her a bit, and when Mary started getting upset, Savoie and Trenton stepped in, and had to convince Abby that she should leave."

Doyle nodded; Trenton was Acton's personal security person, and he was already aware that Lady Abby was trouble, based on past events. The volatile young woman had been engaged to Howard before the man met Doyle's nanny and had fallen instantly in love. Howard had broken off his engagement so as to marry Mary, and Lady Abby hadn't taken it well, at all—in fact, they'd had a previous confrontation with the woman once, when they were holidaying in Dublin.

"Holy *Mother*, Thomas; she's barkin' mad, if she's stalkin' poor Mary still," Doyle breathed, thoroughly dismayed.

Williams nodded. "Savoie said that Mary was embarrassed, of course, and pleaded with the two men not to say anything to you or Acton. He thought he'd drop a word with me, though."

Doyle quirked her mouth. "Poor you, Thomas; you're always on Lady Abby mop-up duty." After the Dublin confrontation, Williams had been tasked with escorting the volatile Lady Abby back to her home in England.

Her companion shrugged. "Not mop-up, this time, as much as I'm Savoie's messenger."

"You did right—both of you."

He nodded. "I don't think Savoie would have mentioned it, if he weren't worried about a potential escalation. Do you think Acton should be told?" This, apparently, was the nub of the reason Williams had wanted to speak with her privately.

Doyle nodded. "Aye, but I'd be very much surprised if Trenton hasn't already told him, no matter the secrecy pledge. Trenton's first loyalty is to Acton, after all, and there's the Sir Stephen angle, too." To further complicate matters, Lady Abby was presently keeping company with Acton's cousin, and since there was no love lost between Acton and Sir Stephen, this latest turn of events—with Lady Abby harassing poor Mary—did not bode well for family peace, if Acton decided to come down like a ton of bricks on the wretched woman.

But Williams shook his head slightly in disagreement. "It's hard to believe Sir Stephen knows anything about it, Kath;

she'd not want him to think she still carries a torch for Howard."

"Oh; oh, I suppose that's true. Not to mention it would reveal that she's mad as a hatter, which may give him pause."

He shrugged slightly. "He probably already knows; it's part of the sex-appeal equation—how crazy is too crazy?"

Doyle made a sound of distaste, as she lifted her cup again, thinking over this new and unwelcome revelation. "Poor Mary; it's such a crackin' shame, Thomas–she's done nothin' to deserve this, except attract a man with a crazed fiancée. And yet again, it's that thwarted-love thing, rearing its ugly head—why can't Lady Abby just take her lumps, and move on? It's not as though she can't attract another man with the drop of a handkerchief."

But her companion only raised a skeptical brow. "I don't know if you'd characterize it as 'love' as much as it's an 'unsound-mind', Kath. I think people like Lady Abby have a pathological disorder, and no one is allowed to reject them."

"True enough. And it's as clear as glass that she's a bit flighty, and prone to temper tantrums, which should be the equivalent of havin' a flashin' warnin' light, atop her head. What is it, with men? Honestly, wouldn't you see it comin' from a mile away, and avoid such a woman like the plague?"

"I think you're underestimating the power of sex-appeal, Kath."

She put her cup down to regard him, thoroughly perplexed. "I think I'd rather not know that men are like robots, with an 'on' switch that doesn't seem to connect to their brains."

"How long have you been working major crimes, Kath?" Williams replied in a mild tone, and then took a sip of his coffee.

"Touché," she conceded, and checked the time on her mobile. "Let's go back; I'm dyin' to hear how Martina's surrender went down."

Recalled to the subject, Williams knit his brow as they rose to leave. "I wish I could go talk to her—go talk to Martina."

Doyle stared at him in surprise as she pushed in her chair. "They're not going to allow a stray DI wander in for a chit-chat, Thomas."

"I know; I know. I'm just so surprised that she's come completely unglued; she doesn't seem the type."

Thoughtfully, Doyle accompanied him out the door. "No, she doesn't—she's made of tempered-steel." She glanced up at him. "But I've seen her more recently that you have, and there was no denyin' that she was startin' to go wobbly. And lest we forget, Thomas; she broke into my flat to murder her wretched husband."

"Right. I'm just so surprised, I guess."

Doyle's hand had started tingling, and so she tucked it beneath her other arm, so as to quiet it. "Another victim of thwarted-love, who's lost her groundin'-tethers because she couldn't live with the fact that her man had strayed."

"It looks that way," he agreed, but he didn't sound convinced. As they headed down the pavement back toward headquarters, he glanced down at her. "So; what's wrong with your hand?"

"I'm not sure," she replied absently.

CHAPTER 7

*D*oyle toyed with the idea of heading on down to Detention herself; Williams' concern about Martina had made her feel a bit guilty. She and Martina were friends, of sorts, and she should be supportive, too—or as much as one was able, when one was a copper dealing with a murderess who was getting herself well-and-thoroughly booked.

She was trying to decide what possible excuse a DCI's wife could use to be underfoot during a surrender, when the idea was quashed aborning by Acton's text message.

"May take some time," it said. "Will meet you at home tonight."

"May handsome trainer come for dinner?" she texted in reply.

"No," he answered back. "Perhaps next time."

Good; he was willing to joke about it, which was certainly a good sign. Hopefully he'd stop drinking and she'd stop lurking about, all secret-like, and being such a baby just because her hand had been going numb, from time to time. Faith, it was miles better already than it was just this morning, and meanwhile she'd been making a mountain out of a molehill and driving her poor husband to drink.

Shame on me, she thought as she made her way over to Munoz's cubicle. No one knows how to handle Acton's black moods better than I do, and I've been handling this one *completely* wrong—as though I've lost what little common sense I have. The cure is to let him know I'm in his corner, no matter what, and to have sex as often as possible—another thing I've been neglecting, lately. Best get crackin'; after all, I'm disabled, and the man may decide he'd like a countess in better working-order.

She crossed her arms atop the wall of Munoz's cubicle. "What's happened with Martina's booking—have we heard?"

Munoz paused in her typing. "Sir Vikili is insisting on a psych-eval, and demanding that she be held in a hospital instead of in Detention."

"Good luck to him," offered Doyle in a dry tone. "The prosecutors aren't going to play games on this one; it's a little too grisly. You almost feel sorry for him—for Sir Vikili, I mean."

"I don't," Munoz replied in a decisive tone. "He's always pulling a rabbit out of a hat, and making the prosecutors look bad. For once, he's run out of rabbits."

But Doyle insisted, "You've got to give the devil his due, Munoz. At least he keeps the system honest, and makes us work for it."

"I suppose," Munoz grudgingly agreed.

It's all very ironic, Doyle thought to herself; because even though Acton is supposedly one of the white-hats, the last thing he truly wants is an honest system. With this thought, her scalp prickled, and she paused to wonder why it would. Of *course*, Acton didn't want an honest system—else he wouldn't be able to skirt along the edges the way he did, and sort things out to suit himself. Not to mention that it might mean that he might be the one, surrendering into custody, someday.

"How's the hand?"

Recalled to the conversation, Doyle lowered her voice. "It's better, Munoz—my hand on my heart. Faith, I hate to even speak of it." This, in a broad hint that mayhap the other girl should stop asking.

Undaunted, Munoz asked, "Have you had it x-rayed? You don't think you should go over and let the Infirmary have a quick look?"

"No," Doyle said immediately. "Then I'd have to tell them how it happened, and I'd rather not."

Munoz made a derisive sound. "Then don't tell them the truth, Doyle—make something up, instead."

"No—I'm not a good liar." Self-consciously, she confessed, "I don't want to get Admin involved, mainly because I don't want Acton to find out I was more hurt than I seemed." She paused, and flexed her hand for a moment. "But if it stops improvin', I'll have it looked at—I promise."

"Don't be the weak link," Munoz warned.

Annoyed, Doyle retorted, "I may not be an alpha-lioness, but I'm not a weak link, Munoz."

"If you say so," said her companion in a skeptical tone. "And speaking of such, Acton asked me to send a forensics team to the D'Angelo construction offices to seize the printer, there. Apparently, Martina was on the premises yesterday, even though the offices have been closed since her husband's murder."

"Holy saints," Doyle exclaimed. "If they can show she printed-up the sign at that printer, it's even more open-and-shut than it was before."

"No psych-eval necessary," Munoz agreed. "Obvious malice aforethought, so no mental hospital for her."

"I'm still worried about whether there are any others—other women she was targetin'," Doyle said thoughtfully. "I get the impression that Antonio was quite the ladies' man."

"I can do a cross-check with unsolved homicides," Munoz offered. "But I doubt Habib will want to spend the money—not without a solid lead." DI Habib was their supervisor, and known to be very careful with his case budgets.

Doyle reluctantly acknowledged this pragmatic aspect of law enforcement—something that was never discussed on the telly's detective shows, where no expense was ever spared. "He'll say it's an unnecessary expenditure, and I suppose he's right; there's no point, since we have her dead-to-rights on this one." Hard on this thought, Doyle knit her brow. "Did you hear that the charge-nurse at the free clinic was murdered, too? Faith, but that place was ground-central for nasty killin's. Do they have an arrest, yet?"

"I don't think so." Munoz grimaced in distaste. "Now, there's an unsound-mind, for you. That poor victim was in the wrong place at the wrong time, and knocked on the wrong door."

Doyle lifted her gaze to thoughtfully review the far corner of the room. "No leads a'tall? That's a bit strange, isn't it? You'd think they'd have a ton of leads, if it happened in the projects."

Munoz shrugged a shoulder. "The flat was 'to-let' at the time, and so they think the killer was a transient. The neighbors had nothing helpful, but that's not so unusual, in that neighborhood. The killer was probably squatting there, was on drugs, and was worried that it was the coppers who were knocking on the door—we're lucky that it wasn't you or me."

Trying to decide why she kept thinking about this particular murder, Doyle ventured, "Is there any chance it was Martina, who killed the charge-nurse?"

Munoz turned to resume her typing, in an obvious signal that she was tired of speaking with Doyle. "Why would Martina kill the charge-nurse, Doyle? It's not as though he was Antonio's lover."

But Doyle persisted, "Her religious Order was goin' after the blacklegs at that smoky clinic, and the charge-nurse was up to his eyeballs in the all-around smokiness."

Munoz didn't pause in her typing. "True, but the charge-nurse was a cooperating witness, remember? They were using his evidence to put together a case against the other players, so Martina wouldn't want to kill him. Besides, whoever the killer was, he was strong enough to drive a sword straight through the victim's chest, so it's unlikely it was a woman." She drew down a corner of her mouth. "You should see the pics–he was skewered like a chicken on a spit."

Doyle lifted her brows. "The transient left his sword behind?"

Munoz nodded. "He did, but apparently it's not much of a lead. It was stolen from a pawn shop."

There was a small silence, whilst Doyle stared at the other girl. "Was—was the pawn shop in Fremont, by any chance?" The Fremont pawn shop had featured prominently in a recent, unrelated homicide—or at least, Doyle thought it was unrelated. Faith, mayhap the pawn shop was like the free clinic, and was serving as some sort of headquarters for the harrowing of hell.

Annoyed that Doyle hadn't taken the hint to leave, Munoz tossed her hair over her shoulder with barely-concealed impatience. "I don't know, Doyle; ask Habib, it's his case, not mine."

"I will. Thanks, Munoz."

In response, the other girl didn't deign to look up.

CHAPTER 8

And now, here's another thing that's bitin' at me, Doyle thought a bit crossly, as she made her way over to her supervisor's cubicle. And I can't get too distracted by the stupid pawn shop popping up yet again, because I've got to go home and sort-out poor Mary's situation, what with Lady Abby's having gone barkin' mad. Oh—oh; mayhap I should first check-in with Acton, to find out if Trenton told him what happened, and ask how he wants to handle it. No —poor Mary will need some soothing, and besides, it's best that everyone in the household be alerted that Lady Abby is on the warpath. And I'd best make sure the building's security people know, so there won't be another mishap like there was last time, when the stupid knockers allowed Martina and her companions to waltz right up into the flat.

Her hand tingled, and Doyle quickly tucked it away to quiet it down, as she halted in Habib's entryway.

"DS Doyle; is your report nearly ready?" Habib cocked a brow at her; Doyle was notorious for untimely reports, being as she wasn't very good at organizing her thoughts at the best of times, and was even worse lately—no doubt due to pregnant-brain. That, and she was married to a famous DCI, which tended to smooth over any and all shortcomings, and therefore make her less-inclined to remedy those very shortcomings.

"DCI Acton requested that DS Munoz prepare the report, sir."

"Ah," the Pakistani man exclaimed in satisfaction, being as Munoz tended to get her paperwork finished in a concise and timely manner.

"It looks to be an open-and-shut, sir—what with the printed-out sign, and all."

"Indeed," Habib agreed with a complacent nod. "We are fortunate."

This seemed a likely opening, and so Doyle decided to venture, "We're not so fortunate with respect to the charge-nurse's murder over at the projects, I hear. I'd be happy to interview the people at the pawn shop, about the sword. I've already been there, a few times."

Habib glanced up. "Officer Gabriel has already interviewed the pawn shop personnel, DS Doyle. Indeed, it was fortunate that he did so, because he was able to identify the sword as Persian in origin." He paused to tilt his head slightly. "Such information gives us a lead, however small."

"Oh—oh, yes, I suppose that narrows the search, sir. A 'four', most likely." The reference was to the police codes that were used as a shorthand to refer to a suspect's ethnicity, and "four" included a suspect who was Middle Eastern in appearance.

But Habib pointed out, "It may have no relevance to the ethnicity of the suspect, DS Doyle. But the weapon is unusual, which is a lead, of sorts. I will send a team to re-canvass the neighbors with this new information; it may help to jog their memories."

"I'll be happy to do it, sir."

But Doyle had forgot that her supervisor was no doubt under strict orders not to allow the pregnant Lady Acton to muck about in the projects, let alone muck about in the projects looking for people familiar with Middle Eastern weapons. Without missing a beat, Habib said smoothly, "Instead, if you would assist DS Munoz with cross-checking recent unsolveds, using this case criteria. The killer may have struck others."

"Of course, sir." This, said with a mental sigh, because there was nothing more tedious than running cross-checks—although she mustn't complain, since this was how they caught serial killers, which was the other, ominous aspect of dealing with an unsound-mind; the killer might be racking-up more victims. "Shall I take a look from the sword end of things? If it's an unusual sword, mayhap we can run down a sales receipt, and ID a suspect."

"The sword was stolen from the pawn shop, DS Doyle," Habib reminded her.

"Oh—oh, right. He's not on tape?"

Doyle could see that Habib—ever polite—was nonetheless rather tired of having to re-explain things to a DS who was not even assigned to the case-team. "It was a smash-and-grab, DS Doyle, and other items were stolen at the same time. The perpetrator wore a balaclava, and there is no identifying information."

"Oh, I see." She knit her brow. "So; we're not certain the transient is a 'four', and we're not certain whether the sword had any particular significance to him. Faith, we can't even be certain that he was the robber, since it sounds like a professional job, and not the type of thing that an unsound-mind could manage."

"Yes," Habib agreed. "The burglary and the murder seem to fit different profiles, entirely. Nevertheless, it is a lead, and so we will follow-up with the neighbors, again."

Although she was aware her supervisor was fast running out of patience, Doyle ventured, "Is there any chance that the charge-nurse's murder is connected to the free clinic case, sir? It just seems such a coincidence—that the cooperating witness happened to be killed by persons unknown. There would be more than a few people desperate to keep him quiet."

The supervisor replied, "Yes–we explored this potential, but the mode of this murder speaks of an unsound-mind, DS Doyle. It would have been far more certain to strike-down the nurse via a professional execution, if the intent was to silence him. And the timing is not right; the witness' testimony had been already taken, so that a containment murder would not accomplish anything."

This all made complete sense, of course, and so Doyle was forced to agree. "Right. Unlikely it's connected, then–unless the murder was nothin' but bare revenge, for grassin' out the others in the pharmaceuticals rig."

Again, Habib tilted his head slightly. "Officer Gabriel mentioned this possibility, when he first recognized the type of weapon. But the only Middle Eastern member of the illegal drugs operation appears to have been Mr. Javid, and we know that Mr. Javid was most certainly dead, at the time of the charge-nurse's murder." With a conscious air, Habib carefully did not look Doyle's way, being as Doyle would know this unfortunate fact better than anyone.

She blew out a breath. "Aye, that. Mayhap the revenge-sword is a happenstance, then; the robbers sold it to the transient because he decided he wanted a weapon."

"Or the transient stole it, in turn, from the robbers."

"There's a good point, sir." Belatedly, Doyle realized that perhaps she shouldn't be discussing Middle Eastern revenge-weapons with this particular supervisor, and so she rose to leave. "Thank you for takin' the time, sir. I'll help Munoz with the cross-checkin', then."

"Very good, DS Doyle."

CHAPTER 9

*T*hat afternoon, Doyle gathered up her rucksack and rang-up the driving service to come pick her up, as it was one of the week-days when she worked from home, for the latter part of the day. Their fancy residential building in Kensington came with a complimentary driving service, and —being as Doyle wasn't an experienced driver—Acton wanted her to use the service, rather than take any chances on public transportation. This was a blessing, actually, since she was never comfortable in crowds, where she was constantly buffeted by cross-currents of emotion. And although she'd been ambivalent about the driving service at first—she was not one who could be comfortable with such a show of luxury—she now appreciated having a few quiet moments of reflection in the midst of her busy days, not to mention the ability to get home to her son as quickly as possible.

Acton had recently installed one of his trusted employees from Trestles as her driver, a young man of Jamaican ancestry who was enjoying his first stay in London. After they were underway, she asked him, "What's the news from home, Adrian? Is Father Clarence still underfoot?"

This, because the Dowager Lady Acton—Acton's disagreeable mother—had taken a fancy to the local Roman Catholic priest, much to everyone's general amazement, and often invited him over to the Dower House so as to join her for dinner. Since the elderly woman was Anglican-aristocrat to the bone, Doyle surmised that she appreciated the priest's amiable good nature, and his willingness to cater to a cross-patch like herself. Not to mention it was a rare country priest who'd be able to resist the offer of the occasional fine meal.

Adrian smiled into the mirror. "I believe he visits often, ma'am. In fact, my mother came across Father Clarence when she was in the village, recently."

Doyle shook her head. "'Tis the eighth wonder of the world, Adrian. Acton best keep an eye out, because the next thing you know, Father will be puttin' up the Stations of the Cross along the long gallery."

With another smile, Adrian observed, "He doesn't seem to be the type, ma'am."

"No, I imagine not—he's not a zealot; not by a long stretch," she agreed. "As a matter of fact, zealots are thin on the ground, in these parts." Unbidden, she suddenly thought of Martina Betancourt, who was herself a zealot, until she'd gone off the rails, all thanks to her miserable husband.

Stop it, Doyle, she firmly commanded herself; do not dwell on Martina and her just desserts. Martina thoroughly deserves her fate, and let it be a lesson; it's exactly what you get for allowing your emotions to override your basic good judgment.

To steer her thoughts away, she asked, "What does our Callie tell you, Adrian? Does she gripe about the workin' conditions here, non-stop?" Callie was the new assistant-nanny, also on loan from Trestles.

The young man flashed his smile again. "No, ma'am. She is happy for the opportunity to stay in London for a while. I've shown her some of the sights."

Why, I believe our Adrian is sweet on Callie, Doyle thought, hiding a smile. And small blame to him; she's a ray of sunshine, not to mention they'd a lot in common. It was rather romantic, actually; they'd already introduced one nanny to her husband–all unknowing–and now perhaps history was repeating itself. Although in this case, Adrian and Callie probably already knew each other, as English villages tended to be very close-knit. Doubly-so, in fact, since it seemed to Doyle that the families who'd served Acton's hereditary estate for generations were fiercely devoted— almost overly-so, as past events had shown. It was all very strange to Doyle, who'd grown up with no vassals to speak of, but who was now hip-deep in them.

She arrived at the flat, and was gratified to see that the aforementioned Callie had managed to stall Edward's nap, so that his mother could perform the ritual of setting the stuffed toys in his bed exactly as he wished, with his favorite dinosaur in pride of place, tucked under his arm. Another adjustment, she thought, as she dutifully kissed the dinosaur, too. Not a lot of dinosaur-speak, when I was growing up, and now I'm being put through my paces.

After a firm admonition that her son go to sleep, he held up his arms demanding that she kiss him one last time before she was allowed to leave.

"How was he?" Doyle whispered, as she shut the door quietly behind her.

"Busy," said Callie with a smile. "But no bones broken."

"The day's not over," Doyle observed.

Her eyes twinkling, Callie replied, "Yes, madam."

"Where's our Mary?"

"She's having a lie-down in the master suite, madam."

"Good; I'll leave her be. You're off for the rest of the day, Callie, and thanks so much."

"Yes, madam; thank you," the girl replied, and with no further ado, headed down to her own room, at the end of the hall.

CHAPTER 10

*D*oyle walked the length of the downstairs hallway, past the stairway, and all the way to the other end to take the lift to the upper floor. When she emerged from the lift it was to see Reynolds, their butler, busy in the kitchen preparing lunch. Because she was pregnant, Acton was gently insistent that she eat a healthier diet than her usual, and so he and Reynolds tended to conspire about such things behind her back. Unfortunately, this usually meant that she was eating miserable egg-and-spinach omelets, when she'd give her right arm for a pasty from a street cart in Dublin— the kind with so much lard plowed into the crust that you had to sit for an hour afterward, just to recover enough to stand upright.

With this unhappy reminder that her vassals tended to conspire against her, she looked over the fruit salad he was arranging, and groused, "For the love o' Mike, Reynolds, don't tell Callie to keep callin' me 'madam' all the time; it gives me the willies."

But Reynolds was unrepentant, as he donned his oven mitts and bent to peer inside the oven's window. "Miss Callie could benefit from instruction, madam, if she is to work in an earl's household."

Doyle dropped into the kitchen chair. "Well, don't crush her spirit, is all."

There was the barest pause. "A good point. I beg your pardon, madam."

With a sigh, Doyle put her elbows on the table and cradled her face in her hands. "No, Reynolds; it's me who should beg your pardon fastin'. Pay me no mind; I've had a rare mornin', and I'm out o' sorts."

"I am very sorry to hear it, madam. Perhaps some green tea?"

Doyle ignored this suggestion as not worthy of a response, and instead lifted her head. "Remember Martina Betancourt?"

"I do, madam."

Of course, he did; Reynolds knew all there was to know about that memorable occasion when the fair Doyle had hurt her hand, and they'd racked-up a body count, right here in the flat. Not to mention that the woman had once attended a dinner-party, here; a dinner-party that had turned into a crackin' Punch-and-Judy show. Doyle's hand began to tingle again, and she tucked it under her other arm to calm it down. "Well, Martina's been arrested for murder, and so she's coolin' her heels in Detention even as we speak."

The servant was understandably confused. "Is that so? I understood Ms. Betancourt was out on her own recognizance, madam."

"No, this one's a new one. She murdered one of her husband's old lovers last night."

Very much shocked, Reynolds paused in opening the oven door. "Great heavens. To think that we harbored a murderer, madam."

Eyeing him sidelong, Doyle refrained from pointing out that Philippe Savoie fit this particular description—as Reynolds well knew—and the Frenchman was constantly underfoot. Look at me, she thought crossly; I'm getting to be all circumspect, and such. "It just goes to show, Reynolds. You never know."

"Indeed, madam."

The servant prepared her plate, and then came around to serve it. "Be careful, madam. It is quite hot."

With a sense of profound wonderment, Doyle beheld a shepherd's pie, the gravy oozing from holes pierced in a light and flaky crust that was browned to a fair turn. "Holy Mother; who are you, and what have you done with Reynolds?"

With discreet satisfaction, Reynolds advised, "Lord Acton suggested you may need something more substantial today, madam, as you've had a difficult morning."

Doyle breathed in the welcome scent and found that she was blinking back tears—faith, she was over-emotional about the slightest thing, nowadays. And it was rather touching, truly; even though she'd been behaving badly, and sneaking about, her husband was nonetheless worried about her well-being, and trying to ease her way. Shame on her, for putting him through it; she'd been neglecting him, and he was suffering for it.

Reminded, she lifted her face. "I was tryin' to remember the name of that famous story, Reynolds; the one where the husband and wife were workin' at cross-purposes."

Reynolds paused to consider this. *"The Mysterious Affair at Styles*, perhaps?"

Doyle rolled her eyes as she began to break up the crust with a fork. "No, Reynolds, they weren't havin' an *affair* in this story; instead they loved each other, but they were workin' at cross-purposes. They gave each other gifts."

"Ah," the butler said. *"The Gift of the Magi."*

Doyle stilled her fork to stare at him. "Why, that's what Acton said. Is that *truly* the name of the story? Whatever for? It has nothin' to do with the Magi."

"The couple were giving each other Christmas gifts, madam."

"Oh. Well, it still seems a strange title, Reynolds."

But the butler bowed his head slightly. "On the contrary, madam; the story is about love and sacrifice. Very appropriate for Christmas, if I may say so."

Doyle re-addressed her pie. "Well, my mother knew all there was to know about love and sacrifice, Reynolds, and the last thing she would have done would be to scrimp so as to give me some gift I didn't really need." Doyle's mother had died a few years earlier, after moving to London with Doyle when she began her training at the Crime Academy. Doyle's father had never been a part of their lives, and her mother had struggled as best she could to keep their heads above water.

"As you say, madam."

Doyle took a tentative bite—the gravy was still quite hot —and then noted, "Acton had the right name for the story, of course, but he'd rather die- in-a-fire than correct me."

"I imagine Lord Acton does not wish to hurt your feelings, madam."

She smiled, slightly, and paused to meet his eyes. "That, or he'd wind up spendin' all his time correctin' me, and doin' little else."

With a wooden expression, the servant refilled her water glass. "As you say, madam."

In some amusement, she insisted, "I do get a lot of things *right*, Reynolds." Again, she resisted the mighty impulse to make a reference to Philippe Savoie; say what you will, she did have a knack for the ferreting-out of plots, be they by husbands, crooks, or wooden-faced butlers.

"You do, indeed, madam," the butler hurriedly agreed, no doubt regretting the tenor of his last remark. "It is uncanny, sometimes."

"That's me," she agreed thoughtfully. "Uncanny."

Thinking this over, she began to eat, and reflected—and not for the first time—that it was uncanny indeed, that she and Acton had wound up married to each other. She was not your ordinary colleen—what with her perceptive abilities, and all—but on the other hand, Acton was not your ordinary aristocrat-turned-detective, either, and her current position as Lady Acton had little to do with any particular merit on her part, but instead had everything to do with the fact that her husband was a bit nicked. Lord Acton wasn't quite right in the head, and so—in between his various plots and masterminding—he'd happened to fixate on a girl who'd passed beneath his window, one day, and that monumental mismatch is what had brought her to her present circumstances, where she was living in a posh flat and having a butler serve lunch. Or "luncheon," as he would say.

Pausing, she reminded herself–a bit sternly–that nothing happened without God's say-so, and that she probably shouldn't be second-guessing; it was a miracle indeed that she and Acton had managed to find each other—they were each the better for it, and shame on her for neglecting the man, lately. She was the center of his universe, and she'd been moping about, instead of assuring him that all was well. Because all was well, of course—or at least as well as it could be.

Mary-the-nanny interrupted her musings, as the young woman emerged from the stairway. "Hallo, Lady Acton; I'm sorry I didn't hear you come in."

Mary was a few years older than Doyle, and they'd met when Mary had served as a witness in a homicide case. Doyle had instantly known—in the way that she knew things —that her own life was intertwined with sweet Mary's, and so she'd promptly recruited the young woman to join their household as Edward's nanny. Mary's husband had unexpectedly died, and so Mary and her stepdaughter had been housed by Acton until she'd met Nigel Howard, an up-and-coming politician who'd fallen instantly in love, even though he was already engaged to be married. Not that anyone could blame him, of course; everyone seemed to fall in love with gentle Mary—even Williams had been sweet on her, for a time.

Mary was now pregnant—a bit further along than Doyle —and so she was not as fast on her feet, nowadays, which was why they'd hired Callie to assist.

Indicating the chair beside hers, Doyle said, "Come have lunch, Mary. You've had your own troubles to bear, and I think Reynolds, here, should be made aware. We need to make sure everyone knows that Lady Abby is not to be given access."

"I am already aware, madam," Reynolds admitted. "Lord Acton felt it necessary."

"Oh—oh, I'm so embarrassed," Mary said, as she covered her face with her hands. "I didn't even want to tell Nigel."

"It's best that everyone be made aware," Doyle advised. "We may have to get a restraining order–we'll see what Acton thinks."

Mary uncovered her face to offer, "I must say I feel a bit sorry for her—for Lady Abby. She must have truly loved Nigel–she's so very upset."

"She doesn't love anyone but herself," Doyle advised in a firm tone. "We see it a lot, in our business; she's an unsound-mind, and I wouldn't be surprised if Acton raps her sharply on the knuckles, to make her mind herself. If she's left unchecked, she may become truly dangerous."

"I doubt Nigel will want a restraining order," Mary ventured. "He'll be worried about the bad publicity."

"He should have thought a bit, then, before he lashed himself to such an out-and-out nutter," Doyle replied with little compassion. "It's a shame, but he can't just sweep her under the rug, and hope to ignore her."

Mary sighed, as she began to address her lunch. "He said she seemed such a different person, before; he's as surprised as anyone."

Men; honestly, thought Doyle. And here's a perfect example of what Williams was talking about, when he said that men tended to focus on one thing, and one thing only. After all, it seems very unlikely that your lady-love would go from not-crazy to crazy at the flip of a switch, with no warnings to be had. Although—although I suppose I have to take that back; Martina Betancourt seems to have performed just that trick.

Her scalp started prickling, but before Doyle could

wonder why this was, she was distracted by Acton's message, saying he wouldn't be home until after dinner. Just as well, she thought, as she absently ran a thumb across the mobile screen; I'll be well-prepared to mend some fences, once the man finally gets himself home.

CHAPTER 11

*T*hat evening, Doyle put Edward to bed, and then sat at the kitchen table, waiting for her husband as she idly watched the steady rainfall out the windows—it was always raining, this time of year. It would be nice to have snow, for a change, instead of all this cold, miserable rain, but she supposed people who had a lot of snow in winter would think she was daft for even wishing for such a thing. It hardly ever snowed in Dublin, which is probably why she'd such fond memories of it. Her mother had loved the snow, even though it meant she'd have to throw another quilt on the bed, and line their boots with newsprint.

Her thoughts were interrupted when she heard Acton's key-card in the slot, and as he entered the threshold, she turned her head to offer a smile; she was determined to be of comfort to him, so that he wouldn't feel compelled to seek comfort from the bottom of a bottle. "I sent Reynolds to bed; your dinner plate's warmin' in the oven."

"Very good," he said, as he hung up his coat in the hall closet. "Have you eaten?"

"I have–I had the remainder of my shepherd's pie, and it was that grand, Michael. Thank you for the welcome reprieve from kale, and other horrid leafy vegetables."

He bent to kiss the top of her head as he passed her, but Doyle wasn't fooled, and suffered a pang; he was worn to a thread, poor man, and the last needful thing was to have him worried about his wife's wonky hand, on top of all the other things he wasn't paid enough to worry about. "I'm sorry I threw you such a wrench, what with my sneakin' over to the physiotherapist. Please tell me you forgive me."

He opened the fridge to pull out the bottle of orange juice, and she realized—with some relief—that he hadn't been drinking, or at least, not recently. Not that he'd had much chance, of course, if he'd been busy playing alpha-lions with Sir Vikili, down at Detention.

"There is nothing to forgive, Kathleen. The fault is mine."

Making a wry mouth, she protested, "For heaven's sake, Michael; it's not your fault that I wasn't honest with you about it, it's my very own, and none other." She blew out a breath, and confessed, "I think I didn't want you to know that I was more hurt than I seemed."

He drank some juice straight from the bottle, and then paused to regard her for a moment. "Has it improved at all?"

"Aye," she replied, mainly because she didn't want to go see a surgeon, but also because it was true; her hand did seem much better than it was, even from just this morning. To demonstrate, she lifted it to show him, and tentatively flexed it. "The trainer seemed to think it was naught too serious, when he showed me the exercises to do."

Tilting his head, her husband suggested, "Perhaps you could invite him here for your sessions, from now on."

This was his not-so-subtle way of saying he'd rather the pregnant Lady Acton not frequent a public gym, and she hastened to assure him, "No—I honestly don't think I need the trainer, any more. I know the exercises, now, and I can tell it's gettin' much better. Truly, Michael; my hand on my heart."

He bent to open the oven door, and she could see that he wasn't inspired by the offerings within. Just as well; it was past time for the wife of his bosom to spring into action.

"You have to eat somethin', Michael," she chided, as she rose to her feet. "I'll make you a ham-and-butter sandwich, if you'd rather." This, in a teasing tone, because Acton wasn't exactly the ham-and-butter sandwich type, and if Reynolds ever heard of it, he'd probably faint dead away.

As she walked past him into the kitchen, she ran a hand down her husband's chest, and said with a great deal of innuendo, "I can pour you a bowl of cereal."

Quickly, he caught her hand, and brought it up to kiss it. "Cereal sounds delightful."

She paused to giggle, because "cereal" was their code word for sex. "Well, you have to eat some actual cereal, first; it's usin' the carrot-and-stick method, I am."

"It is working." He bent to switch off the oven. "Will you join me?"

"I will," she agreed, as she reached to pull the cereal container from the shelf. "And notice that I'm gradually workin' my way back to frosty flakes." The cereal they had on hand was bran-with-raisins; Doyle's personal favorite was frosty flakes, but she'd not partaken of frosty flakes ever since that time they'd been poisoned.

He made no comment–didn't like to be reminded of the whole poisoned-cereal episode, poor man–and she carried over the bowls to the table so as to settle-in next to him. "D'you want to talk about work? Or is it too horrifyin' to contemplate?"

"Too horrifying," he decided, after taking a spoonful.

This wasn't true, which likely meant that he didn't want to talk shop, just now, because his wife was behaving like a wife should, and making broad hints about sex in the offing. But before he could rush her off to bed, she decided she'd best ask, "What's to do about Lady Abby?"

This gave him pause, and he took a breath. "I was hoping you'd not find out."

With a smile, she noted, "Don't be a knocker, husband; I always find out. It's uncanny, I am."

"Indeed, you are," he said with deep amusement, and leaned to kiss her.

"There's a funny word," she offered, pausing because he'd lingered to kiss her, yet again. "You'd think it would mean the opposite of 'canny,' but I don't think it does."

He smiled slightly, and cupped her face with a palm. "Who said you were uncanny?"

"Reynolds. He was tryin' to make me feel better, for bein' such a dim-bulb."

Brushing a thumb over her cheekbone, he said, "Be careful, only."

He was referring to the very real need to keep her perceptive abilities under wraps; all it needed was for the general public to discover that the fair Doyle was a truth-detector—in another age, she'd have been promptly dragged off and burned at the stake.

"I am careful," she assured him. "Ever since my close call

with Commander Tasza, I've been a lot more canny about not lettin' people catch a glimpse of my uncanny-ness."

He was silent, and she castigated herself for bringing up the Tasza subject, right on the heels of the poisoned-cereal subject; she was supposed to be reassuring the man, instead of reminding him about the various close calls she'd experienced.

In an arch tone, she said, "And speakin' of such, I do believe you're changin' the subject; let it be said that I'm wise to your own canny ways, my friend."

He paused, trying to decide what to say, and so she prompted, "I know it's a dicey situation, what with Howard bein' who he is, but we can't just leave Lady Abby to run amok."

"I've made arrangements to speak with Howard tomorrow," he admitted. "We will decide what is to be done."

"D'you think you'll need a restrainin' order?"

Acton tilted his head. "Oftentimes, a restraining order is a trigger."

This was unfortunately true; if the poor victim of harassment was dealing with a person of unsound-mind, service of a restraining order might only incite a rage, with dire consequences. It was always the problem, in this sort of situation; the courts were very careful in doling-out civil restraining orders—lest they be used as a weapon in a broken-up romance, or marriage. But if a restraining order truly appeared to be necessary, there was the very real possibility that it would do more harm than good; instead of being cowed by the court-order, the harasser might become enraged.

"It's a rare tangle-patch," Doyle agreed. "All because Howard couldn't see 'neath the surface–although I suppose most men don't want to look 'neath the surface, when there's a pretty woman, and sex in the offin'."

Acton gathered her into his lap, and bestowed a lingering kiss on her neck. "I looked beneath your surface."

"Only because there wasn't any sex in the offin', Michael —I was too terrified of you." She lifted her chin to grant him greater access.

"It was a conundrum."

"A'course, it was."

He chuckled into her throat. "It means a challenging puzzle."

"And one you neatly solved, with little time wasted," she noted. "Let's go to bed, husband, where you can look 'neath the surface at your leisure."

He pulled away for a moment, to meet her eyes. "Are you certain you are feeling up to it? Tell me the truth, Kathleen."

It was an honest question, and well-meant; her libido had been flagging–as it tended to do, during the first term of pregnancy–but she was filled with a guilty determination to right the marriage-ship, so to speak, and reassure her husband that all was well. Besides, best not let Acton go too long without, since–according to Williams–men had that 'on' switch, and there were plenty of women hoping to switch on Acton's. Shame on her, for letting the poor man drink and stew about his stupid wife and her stupid visits to the stupid trainer.

"Best gird your loins, husband," she teased softly, as she twined her arms around his neck.

He bent his head to kiss her arm. "Have I eaten enough?"

"Two more bites," she instructed, as though she were dealing with Edward.

CHAPTER 12

*B*etter, Doyle thought, as she lay beside her sleeping husband. Everything had been all a'kilter, and now it was better—much better. Maybe that whole just-have-sex-and-don't-look-beneath-the-surface philosophy had some merit, after all. And now Acton was equal parts tired and relieved, and was sleeping soundly. She'd have to see to it that he took better care of himself, lest he fret himself to death.

She wasn't aware that she'd fallen asleep herself, until she was yet again standing on a rocky outcropping, and having one of her dreams. She had them, occasionally—strange, vivid dreams that usually featured someone who'd recently died. Ghost-dreams, where the ghost had a message of sorts for her, but communication was always difficult, and not very straightforward–as though speaking in mere words was rather primitive, and not the preferred method.

Nevertheless, she'd learned to pay attention to these dreams, because the ghost- messages always seemed to be an attempt to ward off coming disasters. Sometimes the ghost was someone Doyle had never met in life, and sometimes the ghost was well-familiar, as he was on this night.

"You, again," Doyle said in surprise. "Haven't they sorted you out, yet?"

Before her stood Dr. Harding, a psychiatrist who'd treated Acton for a short time, until the treatment was revealed to be a frame-up by evildoers, intent on taking Acton down. Dr. Harding had met a bad end, for his sins, but ever since, the psychiatrist had appeared in the occasional ghost-dream in a role that was usually more helpful than not. Doyle surmised that the man was paying his penance, so to speak, and had been tasked with making himself more useful in the afterlife than he'd been in life—a tall order, mayhap, but she kept this thought to herself, being as she wasn't the one in charge.

As was his usual, he was dressed in a fine suit, and—also as was his usual–he regarded her with an impassive expression, as though he wasn't here for the express purpose of having a conversation with her, even though such was obviously the case. In life, his practice had centered on the lofty and well-connected, and therefore someone like Doyle would never have darkened his door. Ironic, it was, that events had thrown them together, and on more than one occasion; between them, they'd managed to resolve a few dire situations, and so she felt they respected one another.

But his first remark caught her by surprise, as he drew his brows together, and fixed her with a steady gaze. "What are you afraid of, Ms. Doyle?"

Doyle blinked, and then joked, "Mayhap I'm afraid of you, Dr. Harding. You did shoot me, once upon a time."

He smiled slightly. "Let's not dwell on the past, shall we?"

There was a small pause. "It's hard not to," she admitted.

Slowly, he nodded. "Yes."

She continued, "It's comin' on Christmas, and I miss my mother. I always do, this time o' year." She paused, and then couldn't help but say, "You're never her; it hardly seems fair."

He nodded again. "Your mother was a strong figure to you; not someone who was easily frightened."

Doyle considered this. "In all honesty," she offered, "I'm sure she was frightened, sometimes, but she never let me see it. I wish I could better hide my feelings; I've sent Acton into the dismals, which is very unlike me."

With another small nod, the ghost agreed. "Yes. You are harboring repressed fear, which is somatic-affective."

After a small pause, Doyle ventured, "That's too high-hat, for the likes of me, Dr. Harding. Tell me what it is you're sayin', in plain terms."

The ghost offered, "You didn't want him to know you were more hurt than you seemed."

She smiled. "Yes—why, that's exactly what I said to Munoz. There, now; there's no need for you a'tall, with all your ten-pound words." Fairly, she added, "Which is just as well; neither one of us should ever go to a psychiatrist, between Acton and me. It would be akin to openin' the Seventh Seal."

"As well I know," Dr. Harding reminded her.

This was, of course, a fair point, but Doyle offered in her own defense, "Well, Acton may come from a long history of unsound-minds, but I don't. My hand's a bit wonky, is all." She paused, thinking this over. "Although you might say that I talk to a lot of ghosts, for someone with a sound mind, so I suppose it's true that we've each got an unsound-mind, when you get technical about it. It's what binds us together, in a strange way."

"Very good," he said.

Doyle frowned at him, uncertain as to what he meant. "It's not as though I can fix it–my–my 'feyness', or whatever you'd call it. Instead, it's my cross to bear."

"A burden," he suggested.

She knit her brow, and lifted her gaze to the distance for a moment—although there was nothing to see but darkness. "No, not a burden—not truly. More like a mixed blessin'—although there are times when I want nothin' more than to crawl under the bed, and hide."

"This morning's crime scene serves as an example."

With some surprise, she brought her attention back to him. "Was I afraid? I suppose I was. I was worried about my hand, and about Acton's drinkin', and the chance that Munoz or Tim might notice either one. But I was just makin' everything worse, in the end; shame on me, for makin' him worry so."

There was a long moment of silence. Why–there's something here, something important, she thought in surprise, but couldn't manage to grasp at the elusive thought. Bringing her brows together, she said to him, "I wish you'd just tell me straight-out what it is you're tryin' to tell me, Dr. Harding."

"That's not how this works," he replied. "I'm afraid you have to sort it out for yourself. But I will ask you again, Ms. Doyle; what are you afraid of?"

With a gasp, Doyle's eyes flew open, and she contemplated the dimly-lit ceiling, waiting for her heartbeat to return to normal.

CHAPTER 13

The next morning, Doyle was preoccupied, as she sat with Edward at the breakfast table. Acton had already left—not only was he was an early-morning person to begin with, he'd a heavy caseload, just now—and so Doyle was using the few minutes of quiet to mull over Dr. Harding's visit, before Callie came upstairs.

As was the usual case when she'd a ghost-dream, she was left with the feeling that she'd best shake her stumps and find out whatever it was she was being prodded to find out. Normally, however, the dreams were connected with a homicide case she was working on—not to mention they usually served as a head's up with respect to some scheme that her renegade husband was masterminding.

This time, though, it seemed a bit different, somehow–the ghost wondered whether she'd been frightened by Martina's crime-scene, which seemed a strange thing to say; a crime scene wasn't frightening—the frightening bits had already happened, and they'd happened to some other poor soul. For someone like Doyle, a crime scene was more like a puzzle—although Martina's puzzle was easily solved. And another thing; the ghost was Dr. Harding, of all people, which also seemed a bit strange, as Dr. Harding had no connection to the case—did he? He was a doctor, of course, but other than that, she couldn't see a link.

Absently gazing out the window, she asked, "Do I seem *afraid* to you, Reynolds?"

The servant paused in lifting Edward's bowl. "Afraid, madam?"

Doyle mused, "I don't think I'm an easily-frightened sort of person, truth to tell."

"Certainly not, madam," Reynolds said with some severity. "Who would say such a thing?"

"Not Acton," she joked. "He's had to hold me back, plenty o' times."

"Indeed, madam," the servant agreed. "You have a very forthright nature, if I may say so." Apparently, the servant decided that the compliment was a bit equivocal, and so he added, "You are also very kind, of course."

She eyed him in amusement, as she rose from her chair. "Doin' it too brown, Reynolds. Mary's the one who's kind—she's the pattern-card for someone with a sweet temper. By contrast, I've a ragin' temper, I do."

"If that is the case, I don't believe I have ever witnessed it, madam," the servant declared stoutly.

With a small smile, Doyle helped Edward down from his chair. "Well, if you'd been here for Martina Betancourt's nasty little holy-show, you'd have seen my temper in all its red-headed glory, my friend."

Delicately, the butler made a grimace of distaste. "Best not to speak of the matter, perhaps."

Doyle led Edward over to the sink, so that she could supervise washing his hands and face. "You forget that I'm Irish, Reynolds–we gabble like geese. You English people are all self-contained, and 'tut-tut,' which is probably why you've lorded it over us, all this time."

"Yes, madam," Reynolds replied, with just the barest hint of disapproval.

"Good morning, madam."

It was Callie, coming up the stairway in her cheerful fashion, and Doyle resigned herself to being "madamed" to death for the next few minutes. "Hallo, Callie. Edward's eaten, and I'll get ready for work. I should be back in time to join you for lunch."

"Very good, madam." The girl hesitated, and then ventured, "I thought I'd mention, madam; Mr. Savoie asked Miss Mary if she would contact him in the event we go over to the park, just so that he could keep an eye on things."

Doyle straightened up to regard her. "Oh—oh, that's very kind of him, I suppose. Is it necessary? Trenton would be there, after all."

"Miss Mary seemed to think it a good idea, but I thought I'd best check in with you."

This seemed properly conscientious to Doyle, being as Callie couldn't yet be certain who was friend, and who was foe. Faith, thought Doyle in mild exasperation; neither can I, for that matter.

She paused, surprised at herself for entertaining such a thought. Slowly, she said, "Let's avoid the park for now, until Acton decides how to handle Lady Abby. Instead, we can let Edward run at Gemma's school, when you go over to pick her up." Gemma was Mary's stepdaughter, and the little girl attended the same school as Savoie's young son.

"Yes, madam."

The girl led Edward off to get dressed, and Doyle watched her, thinking that there'd been a nuance, of sorts, beneath her words. Callie seemed worried about something—was she worried about Savoie, mayhap? There was plenty of good reason, of course, to be wary of the likes of Savoie, but Doyle doubted very much that he'd have done anything in Callie's presence to make the girl nervous—that wasn't Savoie's style at all. Instead, the Frenchman would be all bored and languid, until you realized that–miraculously–things always seemed to work out his way, and sometimes in an alarming fashion.

I'll speak with Savoie, Doyle decided, and winkle out what this is all about. Callie might be young, but she was nobody's fool, and something was making her wary. First things first, though; she'd visit McGonigal's office so as to cast her peepers over that crime scene again. It seemed very unlikely that Dr. Harding had mentioned it for no good reason.

CHAPTER 14

"Going to check-in on Tim," Doyle texted to Acton, as she waited in the lobby for the driving service to pull around. "In case your wondering." She paused, because she wasn't certain if that was the right way to spell "your" in this instance, and so she edited it to say "ur," just to be on the safe side.

As always, his reply came promptly. "Very good. Tell him no further statements needed, if you would."

"Right."

Adrian pulled the limousine to the pavement out front, and Doyle ducked under the doorman's umbrella as he opened the door. "Good mornin', Adrian—although it's not so very good if it's only goin' to keep rainin', every blessed minute. We're off to Dr. McGonigal's office this mornin', d'you know the address?"

"I do, ma'am—Lord Acton just texted me."

"Well, he's Johnny-on-the-spot—I just texted him about it

myself, a minute ago. The man must be lyin' about in his office with nothin' better to do."

With an embarrassed tilt of his head, Adrian confessed, "Lord Acton knew I'd have to check-in, and so he saved me the trouble. Remember when I drove you to that pawn shop in Fremont? Trenton scolded me for taking you there without checking-in, first, and so now I must always inform him if you want to go anywhere other than headquarters."

Doyle considered this, as she gazed out the window. "Who'd win in a knife-fight, Adrian; you or Trenton?"

The young man grinned. "Me," he said.

Doyle shrugged a shoulder. "There you go."

"I'd probably be sent back home, though."

"I suppose that's a drawback, unless you're pig-sick of this place."

Adrian flashed his grin again. "Not as yet, ma'am."

"Best save your powder, then."

Quickly, the young man offered, "I meant no criticism, ma'am; it was a good lesson for me to learn."

Rather than point out that this lesson failed to take into account that she was a seasoned police officer who should be able to decide when she did and did not require back-up, Doyle subsided into silence, and instead considered this interesting little tidbit. That her husband monitored her movements was nothing unusual, but perhaps this wasn't the usual fretting about her safety, and her tendency to rush in where angels feared to tread. The Fremont pawnshop, after all, had served as ground-central for strange goings-on in more than a few of her cases, and now it figured in yet another one, with its stolen sword that had—coincidentally— wound up as a murder weapon. There may be good reason that Acton wanted her well-away from the place, aside from the fact it was located in a gafty neighborhood.

Another thing, on the list of things to check, she decided. It may be nothing, but it may be something, and she should do a "rule-out," just to be certain. And since she didn't want to risk pitching Adrian into a knife-fight, she'd do a work-around, so as to get herself over to the pawnshop without anyone's knowing, and in the process, kill two birds with one stone. Let it be said that her husband wasn't the only wily one, in the family. First things first, though, and this particular first thing was to take another long look at the crime scene at McGonigal's offices.

Once she arrived, however, she was rather surprised to see that everything seemed more or less back to normal, complete with a new office manager manning the desk—a middle-aged woman with an aura of efficiency that reminded Doyle immediately of the Human Resources Administrator at Winchester University.

"Hallo," Doyle said. "I've come to visit Dr. McGonigal—I haven't an appointment, but I'm a friend."

The woman regarded her through her no-nonsense glasses. "Aren't you the policewoman who jumped off the bridge?"

"I am," Doyle affirmed, and pinned on her best humble-hero smile. Doyle had seized the public's admiration by leaping off Greyfriars bridge to save Munoz from drowning, once upon a time, and now she was something of a folk-hero.

"I don't know as I could have done it," the woman admitted. "What were you thinking, when you jumped?"

Since Doyle had been asked this question more times than she could count, she tried to sound sincere as she gave her stock answer. "I wasn't thinkin', truly; I just knew I had to help my friend."

To her great surprise, her scalp started prickling. But why? She and Munoz weren't exactly friends, but the press had played it up as though they were, and so Doyle was more or less stuck with this fictionalized account. The truth was, she'd saved Munoz because she couldn't *not* try to save Munoz, and there was nothin' for it; whether or not the girl was a friend was neither here nor there. Doyle was not one to stand idly by, when someone was drowning before her eyes.

Again, her scalp prickled, as the office manager buzzed McGonigal to announce her visit. Exasperated, Doyle ignored it, because she'd no idea what she was supposed to be understanding—there was not much opportunity to be heroic, nowadays, with another child on the way, and a wonky hand. Besides, she couldn't think of anyone who was in need of saving.

Whilst she was musing over her jumbled thoughts, she remembered to look over the room carefully, and to try to sense whether there was anything she'd missed, here, the day before. She didn't catch a glimmer—faith, the place looked as though there'd never been a grisly murder, in the first place. In fact, the only thing that had made her antennae quiver was the bridge-jumper conversation, where everyone thought it was a devoted friendship that had compelled her to jump, when in reality, it could have been anyone and she'd have done the same, back when she was brave.

Oh, she thought, rather surprised by this errant thought. Am I no longer brave?

The office manager announced, "He'll be happy to see you, Officer Doyle."

"I'm just visitin' as a friend, in this instance," Doyle demurred, and again, her scalp prickled.

CHAPTER 15

*D*oyle could see that McGonigal was a bit apprehensive, as he rose from his desk to greet her, and so Doyle assured him, "Acton says they're finished with you, Tim; I just came by to see how you were doin'."

The doctor smiled a bit ruefully. "Well, that is a relief, Kathleen. Although I feel guilty for feeling that way—that poor young woman. And I know we should pray for Martina, too, but I have to admit I find it difficult."

"Aye, that," Doyle agreed with a stab of guilt. She'd not thought much about Martina—or any of the wretched blacklegs who'd invaded her flat—and the need to pray for their sorry souls. But McGonigal was right; you were supposed to pray for your enemies–that they'd not suffer for their sins, but instead would turn to a better path. Although Martina's path now seemed set-in-stone; she was going to spend a long time in a hard place. Maghaberry, perhaps, in the wilds of north Ireland—although Williams had said that was unlikely, for some reason. Strange, that it kept leaping to mind.

She was aware that McGonigal had asked her a question, and so she returned her attention to him. "I'm sorry, Tim; I was woolgatherin'."

He smiled. "I only wanted to ask how Edward was going on—I haven't seen him lately."

"He's goin' on like a house afire," she declared. "It's exhaustin', is what it is."

The doctor smiled with genuine warmth. "Wait until you've two, to mind."

"We may be forced to surrender, Tim; lucky, we've back-up, to give us a fightin' chance.

"Callie," he nodded. "She came by to see me yesterday, which was a nice surprise, after all the unpleasantness."

Doyle blinked. "Callie did? I didn't know you knew Callie."

"Oh, yes; she broke her arm at Trestles about ten years ago —fell out of one of the chestnut trees, by the old kennel. I was visiting at the time, and so I splinted it up for her."

Doyle smiled at the picture thus presented. "Look at you; you're a knight in shinin' armor, Tim."

Her companion chuckled at the memory. "I was fresh out of residency, and only too happy to do it. She brought me a tin of shortbread—remembered that I liked it."

"Well, she's a very sweet girl, and Edward already thinks she's top o' the trees. Speakin' of which, is your new office manager here to stay, or is she just a temp?"

"She's with a staffing service, and we're trying her out," McGonigal explained. "We have a month to decide, but I've seen no reason not to hire her."

Doyle teased, "Unlikely she's goin' to be castin' her lures

at the doctors, which is probably a good thing, after what's happened to the last one."

"Indeed," he replied, and then lowered his voice to admit, "Which is one of the reasons I chose her, in the first place."

Thus reminded, Doyle asked in an airy tone, "How's our Dr. Okafor? If you think the free clinic's goin' to close, is there any chance she'll wind up workin' with your group?" Doyle knew that McGonigal carried a torch for the African doctor, who used to volunteer with him at the free clinic.

But he shook his head slightly. "No—no; she practices general medicine, and my group specializes in surgery. I do visit with her from time to time, though–she works at Wexton Prison, now."

"Does she? Well, she's on the side of the angels, then." This, because in Doyle's experience, Wexton Prison outdid even the Fremont pawn shop as ground-central for dark doings.

McGonigal nodded. "I am happy for her; she tends to volunteer her services, and so she always seems to live month-to-month. At least at the prison, she'll be well-paid, and have regular hours."

Doyle made a face. "Better her than me; I can't say I have fond memories of Wexton Prison."

He laughed in rueful acknowledgement. "They have fond memories of you, though. And the Prison Ministry there is apparently thriving—Dr. Okafor has signed-on to help."

"Because of course, she has—she'd love that sort of thing." In a strange twist of fate, Doyle had once busted into the prison to rescue the head of the Prison Ministry, and the Ministry now had a robust following throughout the kingdom.

The office manager buzzed, and McGonigal lifted the phone. "Very well; please tell him that I will be straight out."

Thus reminded that she was imposing on the doctor's appointment-time, Doyle rose to leave. "Thanks, Tim–please come by for dinner, soon; Reynolds has been dyin' to cook for someone who appreciates it."

"I will," he agreed, and with a reluctant sigh, straightened his tie as he rose. "I confess I'll be happy to put this entire episode behind me–I always feel as though Sir Vikili is looking to trip me up."

Doyle paused at the door. "It's Sir Vikili, who's here to see you? What's he want?"

"He wants to have a look at the surveillance footage, and ask me a few more questions." He hesitated, seeing her reaction. "Is that all right?"

"Oh–of course it is," Doyle replied. "He's got to try to build a defense case for Martina, and since that's goin' to be a sleeveless task, any tiny wisp would be welcome. It just seems a bit strange that he's askin' for surveillance tape, though; the CID will have it, and they are required to share it with him. It's the law; the prosecution has to disclose all its evidence to the defense team."

McGonigal hesitated. "Do you think I should ask Acton, first?"

Hastily, Doyle disclaimed, "No—no, definitely not; all it needs is to give Sir Vikili a chance to say that the prosecution is tampering with witnesses, or evidence. Just be wary; he's slippery as an eel, that one—don't let him frame you up for the poor girl's murder."

"I'll do my best," he joked. "Although I suppose if I were a prisoner, I'd see Dr. Okafor more often."

They walked out into the reception area, and Doyle could

sense Sir Vikili's extreme startlement upon beholding her, although he hid it well. "Officer Doyle," he said, with a polite nod.

As usual, the Persian man was impeccably dressed in an expensive suit, and his outward expression gave no hint of the turmoil within his breast that had been engendered by the sight of the fair Doyle.

Why, he's afraid of me, she thought in surprise, as she returned his greeting. But then almost immediately, she corrected herself; no–he's not *afraid*, necessarily; he's like Acton, and they don't really know fear. But he's wary, and not at all happy to see me here. I think he may be worried that I've discovered something, but I haven't a blessed clue what it would be—betwixt him and Dr. Harding's ghost, I feel as though I'm missing the boat.

She wasn't sure what else to say; she would have liked to send a message to Martina, since they'd been friends-of-sorts, but it was tricky, because Doyle was law enforcement and Martina was currently cooling her heels in gaol; again, the last needful thing was to give the famous solicitor an opportunity to claim tampering.

And so, she sent no message, but instead retreated back to the waiting limousine with a thoughtful air, wishing she knew why she'd been prodded to come here in the first place. It seemed significant that Sir Vikili had also appeared whilst she was visiting, but—other than the man's suppressed alarm —she wasn't certain what she was supposed to nose out. He was looking for any thread to hang a defense on, and small blame to him—nothing unusual in that.

I'm not sure who would prevail, if Acton got into a knife-fight with Sir Vikili, she mused; although I suppose they engage in mortal combat on a daily basis, when you think about it. And it's a good thing, all in all, that the other side has someone to stand as a check to Acton's manipulations–it keeps everyone more honest, although I suppose a lot of people would wish Sir Vikili weren't such a thorn in our sides. I imagine it all depends on whether he's helping or hurting your cause.

Adrian held the door, and Doyle said cheerfully, "Over to headquarters, please," in her best imitation of someone who was going to stay put at work all day, and had no ulterior plans.

CHAPTER 16

Once back at headquarters, Doyle logged in to her computer, and then rummaged around in her top drawer for one business card in particular. Once she had it in hand, she slid her mobile phone into the desk drawer, and then cast her gaze over the sea of cubicles, looking for an empty one. There; over by the far wall, which was perfect.

Casually, she walked over and ducked in to use the desk phone, quickly punching in the international phone number that was displayed on the card.

"*Oui?*"

"Philippe, it's me. Are you free anytime today? I need you to drive me somewhere."

"*Bien.* An hour?"

"Thanks."

She rang off, and quickly stood to retreat back to her own desk. There was nothin' for it; she needed to take a gander at the stupid pawn shop on the sly, and she also needed to speak to Savoie about the Lady Abby altercation, so she may as well pair up the two projects. Savoie had served as her driver once before, when she'd slipped the leash, and therefore he knew to meet her at an intersection a few blocks away.

Because she had a bit of time before she ducked out, she decided to do some follow-up on the other side of the pawn shop case, so to speak, and see if she could winkle-out some information about the charge-nurse's murder, since she couldn't seem to shake the feeling that there was something significant, here, that was hovering just out of reach. To this end, she wandered upstairs to where the higher-ups had their offices, and tapped on Officer Gabriel's door jamb.

The young man was reviewing something on his computer, and looked up at the sound. Tall and slender, he had the casual air of someone who didn't take anything very seriously, which Doyle knew was actually the front for a very keen mind. He'd been in MI 5 before his present position at the CID, and Doyle felt that it wasn't at all clear what that position actually was—whether he was on loan, on some sort of task force, or had been transferred permanently. In any event, they'd shared an adventure or two, with Doyle very much appreciating the young man's talents and sense of humor—he'd helped her out of a few tight corners, and in turn, she'd done the same for him.

"Hallo, Gabriel; d'you have a minute for a consult?"

He gestured her in. "I do, as a matter of fact. How's my favorite baroness?"

Doyle slung down her rucksack, and settled into one of the chairs. "I'm a countess, now. You're not keepin' up."

"Technically, I think you're both."

Doyle confessed, "I don't know how it works; I truly don't think about it much."

"And that's why you're my favorite baroness."

She smiled, and then leaned forward to ask sincerely, "How are you, Gabriel? You've had a tough go, and I'm that sorry."

He shrugged in acknowledgment. "I've had better years."

This was unfortunately true, as Gabriel had been shot, sent to rehab for a drug addiction, was passed over for promotion, and had abruptly lost his girlfriend—the fair Munoz—to her current husband. In an encouraging tone, Doyle offered, "You've been snake-bit, my friend, but things will turn around, now. Better days lie ahead."

"Don't jinx me," he cautioned. "It's hard enough to stay off the window ledge, as it is."

To Doyle's relief, this was not true, and he did seem to be in good spirits. She ventured, "Are you in some sort of program? Can I be a helper, or whatever it's called?"

"Sponsor," he supplied with a smile. "And I appreciate the offer, but I'm taken care of. I will say that I wish there was a twelve-step program for the lovelorn."

In an encouraging tone, Doyle assured him, "You'll find someone, Gabriel—a handsome boyo like you, and smart as can stare."

"Well, I don't know about the staring part, but I am seeing a nice girl. This time from my own gene pool."

Doyle raised her brows, as that gene pool was Persian. "Nazy?"

He raised his own dark brows in return. "And who is Nazy?"

"Oh. She's Acton's assistant, and she needs someone to distract her from Sir Vikili's *beaux yeux*."

"Ah. He's my main competition in the gene pool, it seems.

Marjan would throw me over in a second, if Sir Vikili dropped his handkerchief."

Doyle smiled. "Tell me about the fair Marjan."

He shrugged. "Nice enough."

"Now, there's faint praise."

He cocked a brow at her. "I'm changing my strategy, because everyone I'm mad for either winds up dead or married to an Irishman."

She made a sound of sympathy. "You'll come about, Gabriel. And I don't mean to sound uncarin', but could I interrupt our little heart-to-heart to ask about a case?"

"Certainly. I stand at your disposal."

"It's about the charge-nurse murder, in the projects."

"Unsound-mind," he declared, wincing. "We've got extra surveillance on the area, now, because we're terrified he's going to do it again."

Doyle raised her brows in alarm. "You don't think it's a one-off, then?"

Slowly, he replied, "I'm worried that it's not. It was too happenstance for my taste, which makes me think we may have a seral killer. The housing unit where it occurred was empty, so the perp is presumed to have been a transient, waiting for someone to cross his path."

Doyle nodded, as unfortunately this happened, from time to time; an unsound-mind would lie in wait for the next unlucky person to pass by and get murdered, all for being in the wrong place at the wrong time. "Any leads based on the weapon? We can trace it to a pawn shop burglary, I hear."

In a skeptical gesture, Gabriel raised a palm. "Unlikely my perp is the same fellow as the pawnshop robber; that burglary looks to have been done by a professional. More likely my perp got the sword from a fence, or he may have even killed the robber so as to take the sword—another concerning possibility. I checked with the Met's burglary team, once I discovered the connection, but they're having trouble finding any leads for me, and none of their usual-suspects has been killed, as far as they know. In particular, I asked them to look for 'fours,' because the weapon was Persian."

Doyle frowned, thinking this over. "Habib said it's hard to know if that's significant, though. He may not have been a 'four,' but may have just liked the sword."

Gabriel shrugged. "Could be."

Feeling that she hadn't been very encouraging, Doyle hastily offered, "Good work, though, on identifyin' the murder weapon as the same sword that had been stolen; at least they've a lead, of sorts."

"It's not the type of weapon you see every day." He paused, eying her speculatively. "Are you here to tell me you have a hunch? Because I'd love to roll this fellow up, before he does it again." Gabriel was well-aware that Doyle's "hunches" were usually spot-on.

With no small regret, she shook her head. "No—mainly, I was curious about this one, because the victim was a witness in my free clinic case—the one with the illegal pharmaceuticals. The charge-nurse was grassin' out all the other blacklegs, but Habib is skeptical that there's a connection between that case and his murder."

Slowly, he nodded in agreement. "I'm skeptical, too; I don't see a connection—it looks like a 'random' if I ever saw one. Besides, if the brass thought there might be a connection, they would have handed this case back to Williams, since he was the CSM on the clinic case."

"There's a good point." She paused, wondering again

why she couldn't seem to stop dwelling on the charge-nurse's murder. "It just seems such a coincidence, that the charge-nurse grassed out the evildoers, and how he's been run through in such a nasty fashion. Acton always says that he doesn't believe in coincidences."

Considering this, Gabriel leaned back in his chair. "A revenge killing? I suppose it's possible, but the manner and mode doesn't lend itself."

"Aye," she reluctantly agreed. "It does seem a bit too happenstance, for a retribution murder. And I suppose you're right; if there was any hint of a connection to the clinic case, they've have handed it over to Williams, instead of you."

At the mention of Williams, her companion cast a speculative eye her way. "And how is Williams? Marjan tells me that rumors abound he's shacking-up with Lizzy Mathis, from Forensics."

Nonplussed, Doyle stared at him, trying to decide what to say.

Seeing her distress, he chuckled, and held up a hand. "Don't worry, I won't extract an answer."

"Sorry," she said. "I'm just not sure that the tale is mine to tell." Crossly she added, "I hate it when everyone skulks about. Why can't people just be honest about everythin'?"

He laughed. "Because then we'd be out of a job, Sergeant. And—speaking for myself—I get into too much trouble, when I'm idle."

"Idle hands are the devil's workshop," she agreed. "Although it seems that busy hands are equally to blame—greedy hands, in particular."

"It all probably depends on the devil's manner and mode," he suggested.

"More like his motive and opportunity," she replied with

a smile, and then checked the time. "I've got to run, but thanks for the consult—although it's not my case, so I suppose I can't call it a consult."

"My pleasure," he said, as he turned back to his work. "Let me know when you solve it."

CHAPTER 17

a short while later, Doyle hunched her shoulders against the cold, and waited for Savoie at the designated intersection a few blocks away from headquarters. She'd stepped back to stand beneath a tree, because she'd forgot her umbrella, and it was looking to rain, again. That, and she was hoping she'd managed to avoid any sightings on the CCTV cameras in the area, just in case. She loved her husband, but he was a wily one, and it would be nice if this unauthorized outing never saw the light of day. She shouldn't be mucking about in Gabriel's case—especially without telling him—and with Acton's being the Senior Investigating Officer, to boot. Not that Acton wouldn't save her bacon if she was caught out, of course; he was her champion, although there were times when she wasn't at all certain that his championing of the fair Doyle was an unmixed blessing.

It could be worse, she admitted with some humor; at least there was no chance of any thwarted-love problems, with

MURDER IN UNSOUND MIND

such a devoted husband. Instead, she'd a heaping helping of the exact opposite—un-thwarted love, if there was such a thing, rushing through her life like a raging river, and the devil take the hindmost. She'd a tiger by the tail, as her mother used to say.

With a pang, she decided that she didn't want to think about her mother, just now, and so she turned her mind to Gabriel, and what a relief it was that he seemed to be on the road to recovery. He'd weathered the storm with his sense of humor intact, and even though they'd been joking about it, thwarted love was often the trigger for a deepening spiral of depression and unsound-mind. They saw it a lot, in this business; jealousy caused the perpetrator to go off the deep-end, and lay waste to the people who were the source of his or her torment. As an excellent case-in-point, Martina Betancourt loved her husband so much that she killed him, and then—no doubt conflicted about the terrible thing she'd done—she went off on a jealous rampage to kill all his assorted lovers, for good measure. An unsound-mind, in spades.

Her scalp started prickling, and so she paused to examine this last thought. Williams had been very surprised by Martina's latest murder, and in a way, he was right—Martina was the last person you'd think would go thwarted-love crazy, save for the inarguable fact that Doyle had been a first-row witness to this unfortunate turn of events. The woman had killed her husband, and then had run amok, killing his lover for good measure.

Back at the beginning, when she'd first started working with Acton, he'd explained that humankind had a set number of predictable reactions to certain stimuli, and so it was the detective's job to understand this, and look for those reactions. It had proved very true; they saw a lot of the same patterns in detective-work, which was one of the reasons the CID had half a chance—they knew who tended to be the suspects, in any given case. Which was important, for some reason, save that she'd no idea why that was.

Tired of getting signals which seemed too obscure for her poor brain to decipher, she put her injured hand beneath her other arm, and began to do her flexing exercises beneath her coat.

Savoie was a few minutes late, as was his custom; he was a cautious, careful man, was Philippe Savoie, which was how he managed to survive as a criminal kingpin—although she shouldn't truly call him that anymore, in all fairness. She'd the general impression that he'd rolled his questionable operations way back, ever since he'd adopted his young son. Not to mention that around the same time that he'd adopted his son, he'd formed some sort of shadowy alliance with the fair Doyle's wedded husband. It wouldn't behoove Savoie to jeopardize a shadowy alliance with the renowned Chief Inspector, and so it seemed he was making a determined effort to fly beneath the Met's radar, and turn a more respectable leaf. A good thing; it would cause no end of embarrassment, if Acton was called upon to bail Savoie out of Maghaberry Prison.

A late-model black car pulled up, and she hurried over to open the passenger door and slide in. "Thanks, Philippe; I'm that grateful to you."

"*C'est rien.* We go to the prison?" He was half-joking, because they'd taken an unsanctioned trip to Wexton Prison on a long-ago occasion, when she'd walked headlong into a trap, like a culchie wearing his suit backwards.

"As much as I'd love nothin' more than to re-create that horror-show, Philippe, this time I'm wantin' to go to a pawn shop in Fremont—I have the address."

He raised his brows, and she could sense his surprise. "*Oui?*"

"Yes. I have to make a short visit, and I'd appreciate it if you didn't mention it to anyone." By anyone, of course, she meant Acton, which he would understand without her having to say it. Savoie was fond of her, and they had a strange sort of friendship, arising from the time when he'd decided to save her life even though it wasn't in his best interests to do so. He'd proved loyal in the past, and she knew—in the way that she knew things—he'd prove loyal now.

"*Bien,*" he said and paused for a moment. "You have need of *l'argent*, perhaps?"

"If I knew what that was, I'd tell you."

He rubbed his fingers together. "The money. You have need of the money?"

She smiled. "No, I do not. If I had need of the money, I'd only ask Acton, and he'd hand over as many fistfuls as I wanted, with no questions asked."

"And me," he insisted, a bit affronted. "I would give the fistals, *aussi.*"

"Well, I appreciate it, Philippe, but you should mind your pennies; you have Emile, now, and the tuition at St. Margaret's is not for the faint of heart."

"*C'est vrai,*" he acknowledged, with a small smile.

Suddenly struck, Doyle asked, "Isn't Emile due for a birthday, soon?"

He bowed his head. "Last week. *Mercredi.*"

Aghast, Doyle stammered, "Oh—oh, Philippe, I forgot,

and shame on me. I've been—well, I've been mopin' about, and distracted. I beg your pardon fastin'."

Her companion shrugged. "*De rien*; Marie brought him a gift and—" here, he made a gesture in the air indicating balloons—*les ballons*, when she saw him, after school."

Doyle frowned at him. "Who's 'Marie'?"

Patiently, he explained, "Your nanny, yes?"

"Oh—oh Mary. Yes, that's very like her to remember, and it makes me feel even worse. Tell me what he'd like as a gift, and I'll have Reynolds bake him a cake, because such a thing is beyond my capabilities."

"Puzzle books," Savoie said promptly, and with no small pride, "Emile, he is *très intelligent*."

"I wish I was. I'm so sorry."

He tilted his head in understanding. "You must not worry, little bird. You have had the *malchance*."

There was a nuance to his tone, and she sighed. "I suppose you've heard all about the donnybrook at the flat."

"*Oui*," he said. "I am not surprised you are *la héroïne*, but I am surprised that Martina would do such a terrible thing."

Doyle was reminded that Savoie had known Martina fairly well, and agreed, "Aye; but I suppose you never know when someone's going to shift off their pins–she was aimin' to kill her husband in a state of grace, and nothin' else mattered. And speakin' of such things, I wanted to ask you about Lady Abby, and what happened the other day at the park."

His demeanor did not change, but she could sense that he grew wary. "Yes?"

"Well, we may have to file for a restrainin' order, and I just wanted to make sure I have my facts right. You were there?"

"*Oui*," he said, and offered nothing more.

"Who else?" she prompted.

"*Bien*. Trenton, Callie, Emile, Gemma, Edward."

He rattled off the names in the manner of someone who was used to giving the police only as much information as he deemed necessary, which caused Doyle to eye him thoughtfully. "Well, how did Lady Abby know Mary would be there, at the park? D'you think Lady Abby was spyin' on Mary?"

"I know not," he said.

This was true, and so Doyle ventured, "D'you think she's dangerous—that she'll do it again?"

Savoie, of course, had his own fine-tuned sense, sharpened from many years of dealing with dangerous people, and so he cocked his head, and seemed to think this over. "*Non*," he decided, and—to Doyle's relief—this was true.

"Well; thank you for steppin' up, my friend; Mary says you and Trenton came to her rescue."

"*De rien*," he replied, in all modesty.

Doyle watched through the windscreen for a moment, as they began to drive through the seedier part of town. Not good, she thought; she'd the impression that Callie was wary of Savoie, and Savoie definitely wasn't saying all that he knew about the confrontation. It didn't make much sense, though; mayhap Callie had been shaken-up by Savoie's manner, or something—he was definitely not your warm-and-fuzzy type, and mayhap he'd acted a bit overly-menacing with Lady Abby. She should raise the subject with Callie—although it would be a tangle-patch, to try to explain to the girl that Savoie was a harmless sort of criminal kingpin.

She watched the scenery out her window, and made no further comment as they continued the journey to the Fremont pawn shop.

CHAPTER 18

$\mathcal{S}$avoie parked his car in the no-parking zone in front of the pawnshop, and Doyle explained, "You don't have to come in, if you'd rather not. I just have to ask some questions about a burglary, and it shouldn't take long."

"I will come," Savoie decided, after taking a look at the steel-gate-protected windows, and the graffiti on the walls. "I will find a gun to buy, *peut-être*."

"They're not allowed to sell guns, Philippe," she reminded him, as she stepped out of the car.

"Ah," he said, as though he was humoring a small child. "*Quel dommage.*"

Making a wry mouth, Doyle nonetheless instructed as they approached the door, "Just don't be scarin' the poor man; I need him to answer my questions."

"*Bien,*" he agreed. "I will look to see if they have books for Emile."

They walked into the store, which was manned by a reedy young man who looked up from reviewing his mobile phone.

There was no one else in the store, as the weather did not lend itself to foot traffic.

"Good mornin'," said Doyle as she showed her warrant card. I was wonderin' if you could answer a few questions about the burglary, here."

The young man straightened up, and scratched his arm. "Which one?"

"Oh. The one where the sword was stolen; it was used as a murder weapon in a subsequent crime."

"Right." He nodded, and then offered up a shy smile. "Officer Gabriel came to ask about that one."

"Indeed, he did; I'm just here for a bit of follow-up."

"Oh. Right, then. You haven't caught him, yet—caught the murderer?"

"Not as yet; we're followin' up on some leads." She paused, and then decided there was nothing for it, and she may as well ask, "Are we certain the suspect was a man, and not a woman?"

The fellow looked as though he felt a little sorry for Doyle, being as she was so very ignorant, and nodded. "Oh yes. Even though he wore a balaclava, you could tell it was a pretty strong guy. He was about his size." With a nod, he indicated Savoie, who stood at the other end of the shop, reviewing the children's books that were jumbled on a makeshift shelf.

"I haven't seen the tape, as yet," Doyle confessed. "If it was a man, did he appear to be Middle Eastern—could you tell?"

The young man shrugged. "I dunno, but Officer Gabriel thought that it was likely the suspect had come in to survey the place ahead of time, and so we both looked over the footage from the week before. He asked if I remembered anyone with a scar on his face."

Doyle stared at him in surprise, because it was irrefutable that Philippe Savoie sported a nasty scar across his cheek. Nonsense, she immediately scolded herself–for heaven's sake, Doyle; you're jumping at shadows. If the robber was Savoie, he'd have never walked in here, bold as brass.

With a sinking heart, she admitted to herself that this was not exactly true, and so—with a mighty effort—she smiled at the young man. "Did Officer Gabriel have a suspect in mind, then? I'm afraid I haven't read all his notes." This, said in the conspiratorial manner of one who is aware that she wasn't doing as good a job as she ought, which was often a useful tack to take with a witness of this ilk. Not to mention it was the truth, of course, and Doyle was fast-coming to the realization that she may have stepped into a massive tangle-patch, all unknowing, which seemed to be her normal state of affairs whenever she enlisted Savoie to help her.

"He didn't say." Since they were being conspiratorial, the young man leaned in to disclose. "But Officer Gabriel's a gamer, like me, and a big fan of *The Warlock Wars*. He gave me some tips about advancing to level thirteen."

"Officer Gabriel's a knowin' one," Doyle agreed, and managed to resist the urge to press her palms to her temples. Doggedly, she remembered another question. "What else was stolen—did it seem that the perp was after anythin' in particular?"

The young man shrugged in the jaded manner of one for whom robberies were a commonplace. "It was a smash-and-grab, in the jewelry case. But I told Officer Gabriel that the guy chose the wrong day for a burglary, because there wasn't much in the case that was worth anything—a fake necklace, and some cheap rings—mostly rubbish."

Doyle regarded him for a silent moment. "I see—so it was a jewelry heist. But then he also took the sword? The sword that was the murder weapon?"

"Yes–we'd just got it in, and I put it on display, hanging over the door. He must've seen in on the way out, and grabbed it, too." He smiled slightly. "It was something like; had a lot of cool writing on it, etched along the blade—I would have wanted it, myself. Officer Gabriel said it was really old."

"Thank you," Doyle said in the manner of one who is winding up an interview. "I'm sorry I made you go over old ground."

"No problem," he said cheerfully, and went back to his mobile phone, which was very much appreciated, since Doyle's main task at this point was to get Savoie out the door without the clerk taking a gander at his scar—although Doyle didn't put a lot of faith into the young man's observation skills, which was a helpful thing, for a change.

As she headed out the door, Doyle wished she knew how she was going to broach the subject of felony-burglary with the very felon who'd kindly offered her a ride to the scene of the crime. Fortunately, she was to be spared this calculation, because as he emerged into the cold daylight, it was to behold Acton's Range Rover, with Acton himself leaning against it, his hands in his coat pockets as he watched her emerge from the store.

CHAPTER 19

*D*oyle regarded her husband for a moment, and felt a twinge of conscience; the poor man had a free-range wife, and it was driving him to distraction.

"May I drive you?" he asked.

"You may," she decided. "But I'll have some straight answers from you, my friend."

He opened the door for her, and offered deferentially, "In the future, perhaps you could bring your mobile with you, and instead tell me that you'd rather not be traced."

She had to smile at this patently unworkable option. "You wouldn't be able to resist, Michael; especially if I hinted at secret doin's." She sighed, as she settled into the seat. "I'm sorry I gave you the slip—I know you worry."

"No—the fault is mine, that you felt you had to go to such lengths."

He closed her door and came around, and as he started up the car she offered, "Just to skip over this part, let's compromise, and say the fault is both of ours. Please don't blame Savoie, though; he was only followin' orders. And small wonder he jumped ship–I made him return to the scene of the crime, after all."

She eyed him in a pointed manner, and Acton tilted his head in one of his patented non-verbal acknowledgements, being as he rarely ever confessed to any of his many and varied machinations. "What did he tell you?"

"Oh no; we're not playin' that game, husband. You will tell me what's afoot here, instead."

He considered this for a moment, as he navigated through the mid-morning traffic. "I don't know as I should."

She let out an exasperated breath. "Well then, let me get the ball rollin'; you wanted your stupid sapphire necklace back, and for whatever reason you didn't want anyone to realize that you'd taken it."

This was actually not a difficult leap of logic to make; the "fake" necklace that the clerk had referenced was actually genuine, a valuable antique adorned with rare sapphires that had been used to bait more than one Acton-trap. Apparently, he wanted it to come home again with no one the wiser, and so Savoie had been enlisted to do a bit of smash-and-grab, which was technically below his water-level, nowadays, since he'd graduated to major crimes quite some years ago. Faith, it must have seemed like old times, to him, to do something so petty.

Again, Acton tilted his head, and voiced mild disagreement. "The necklace is yours, technically."

She blew a tendril of hair off her forehead. "Well I don't want it, because it belonged to horrid Mr. Javid, and I wouldn't be at all surprised if it was crackin' bad luck, when you think about how it featured in the Rizzo case, not to mention the wretched Code One at our flat."

"A fair point," he conceded. "It may indeed bring bad luck to its owner."

She glanced at him sidelong, because she thought she detected a nuance in his tone. "I don't think you believe in luck, whether good or bad."

"I had the best of luck when I married you."

She made a face, and turned to gaze out the windscreen. "It wasn't luck, as much as it was stealth and sleight-of hand, my friend. And don't think that I can't see that you're tryin' to divert the topic away from your well-deserved scoldin', husband. Next you'll be tryin' to sweeten me up with hints about daytime sex."

There was a small silence. "That hadn't occurred to me, but I confess you've caught my attention."

"Fine," she agreed in an exasperated manner. "Let's go home; you've forced my hand."

With no further ado, he turned at the next corner. "Speaking of which, how does your hand?"

"It's gettin' better," she replied, and lifted it to demonstrate. "I forget it's even hurt, sometimes. But before I get distracted, I should mention that I think Gabriel has twigged you out. He was askin' the clerk if there was a man with a scar in the shop recently, scoutin' it out."

"Was he? That is of interest."

She nodded. "Gabriel's a wily one. Not as wily as you, but he's on the podium. Don't let him roll you up on a petty crime like this one, for heaven's sake—it would be beneath you."

"A humiliating comeuppance," he agreed.

Turning on him, she scolded, "It's not funny, Michael. Faith, that's all we need, to put the capper on this miserable year. I'd have to bring-in Edward to visit you in prison, and I feel sorry for the guards, already."

He reached to take her hand. "Perhaps we should go on holiday, instead of prison. Somewhere warm, like Bermuda."

She looked over at him in surprise. "It's comin' on Christmas, Michael. You're supposed to stay home, at Christmas."

"Perhaps Trestles, then. Shall we spend Christmas at Trestles?"

She blinked, as this request was unexpected. On the other hand, her husband loved going to Trestles, and a change of scenery might be just the thing to help cast off her doldrums —not to mention they'd be waited on, hand and foot. No point in having vassals, one would think, unless you put them to good use, now and then.

As she watched the rain begin to spatter on the windscreen, she asked, "Does it snow, there?"

He considered this. "About the same as here—not very often."

She blew out a breath. "Now, there's a shame. It would be fun to see Edward handle the snow."

"It would indeed. Think on it, only; we needn't decide immediately."

"Aye, that—although I suppose if we stayed here in town, we'd be forced to fend for ourselves, since all the various Trestles recruits will go home for Christmas."

"A good point," he agreed. "Our very survival may hang in the balance."

In an encouraging tone, she said, "We'd manage, Michael; we only need to have Reynolds stock up on tinned food, and then show us how to operate a tin-opener."

"You paint a very bleak picture," he observed.

They turned onto their street, and Doyle admitted, "It would be temptin'—to go off into a time-warp, and loll about for a few weeks, without a care in the world."

"Only say the word. I will inform Hudson to make preparations, and assemble staff."

Reminded, Doyle turned to him. "Callie went all on her own to visit Tim; I was that surprised."

"Yes. They have known each other quite some time."

Her antenna quivered, and she stared at him in abject surprise. "Holy Mother, Michael; never say you're *match-makin'*?"

He smiled at the suggestion, as he turned into their building's parking garage, and nodded to the guard. "Nothing so heavy-handed. I only thought he could use a distraction, to cheer him up."

Doyle could only agree with this basic truth. "Nothin' like a pretty lass to lift a man's spirits, and his poor spirits deserve a bit of liftin', after everythin' that's happened." Thinking about this development, she had to smile. "Faith, I'd have never pegged you for a hopeless romantic, Michael."

He smiled as he parked the car in the designated slot. "Oh? I would think it obvious."

She laughed heartily, and the sound almost startled her, because she hadn't laughed heartily in quite some time. "Well, I can see your fine hand behind the whole Williams-and-Lizzy semi-marriage, so don't even try to deny it. Although in that case you weren't matchmakin' as much as hittin' him over the head and trussin' im up in a sack." She considered this for a moment. "It was very similar to what happened to me, when you think about it."

Acton, of course, was not going to admit to any of this,

but only offered in a mild tone, "I only thought to remind McGonigal that he was not unattractive to the fairer sex."

Doyle cautioned, "Well, that's a dangerous thing to dabble in, Michael; let's not forget that some fair-sex people are too attractive for their own good, with Lady Abby comin' immediately to mind. Did you and Howard decide what's to be done?"

"We did meet to discuss that matter," he replied.

Although the words were said in a neutral tone, Doyle caught a quick sense of grimness, and so she stared at him, thoroughly alarmed. "Oh-oh; what's to do?"

"I am not at liberty to say, unfortunately."

As this was completely unexpected, she contemplated him in surprise. "There'll be no restrainin' order, then?"

"No."

As he offered nothing further, she ventured, "Never say that Howard still has feelings for her?"

"No. But I am not at liberty to say more. He assures me that he will see to it that she does not contact Mary any further."

Doyle gave him a skeptical look, as she opened her car door. "Good luck, tellin' an unsound-mind what to do."

CHAPTER 20

*a*fter a hurried and robust round of midday sex, Doyle lay sleepy in her husband's embrace, and wasn't aware that she'd dozed off until she stood once again on the blustery outcropping, facing Dr Harding. And although this seemed a bit intrusive—given the midday sex, and all—Doyle was not unhappy to see him, since she'd a bone to pick.

"Why was I sent over to the pawn shop, for the love o' Mike? It was crackin' awkward—I'm supposed to be an LEO and there I was, bringin' Savoie back to the scene of the crime like a first-year dosser. And then for the topper, I run into Sir Vikili at Tim's office, which was that awkward, since he's goin' to lose this round to Acton, thanks to his wretched client's not bein' able to control her murderous impulses—"

"A bit more slowly, please," Dr. Harding interrupted. "Don't forget to breathe."

Dutifully, she took a breath, and tried to rein in her racing thoughts. "Sorry. I can feel that somethin's there—there's somethin' strange in all this, but I can't concentrate long enough to ferret-out whatever it is."

"It will come," he said in an encouraging tone. "Try not to be impatient."

"I'm not the patient sort," she explained, almost apologetically. "Acton is, but not me."

"Exactly," he said. "Very good."

She bit back a sharp retort—being as he wasn't being very helpful at all—and instead mused aloud, "I feel a bit sorry for her—for Martina, I mean. I'd like to send a message, but I can't, bein' as I'm an LEO, and she's sittin' in the nick."

The psychiatrist nodded. "Yes. Very good."

Doyle stared at him for an irritated moment. "What's 'very good,' and why d'you keep sayin' it? You're that annoyin', and you're *never* my mother."

"Now, now," Ms. Doyle, he soothed. "Let's stay on-topic, shall we?"

She blew out a frustrated breath. "Faith, I haven't a flippin' clue what the topic is, in the first place."

"You went to the pawn shop, and you are unhappy with me about it, for some reason."

"Well—yes. I'm gettin' my cases mixed-up, though—you didn't send me to the pawn shop, you sent me to Tim's office. I know Martina's case doesn't have the first thing to do with the sword from the pawn shop, but I just got the idea—the idea that—"

"Yes?" he prompted, into the silence.

She closed her eyes briefly. "I can't remember, but it was one of my feelin's."

He was silent, and Doyle frowned, thinking it over. "The new office manager at the crime scene made a remark about

how I saved Munoz because she's a friend, but that's not true
—not really. I would have tried to save anyone."

Dr. Harding peered at her over his spectacles. "And has
that changed?"

She regarded him in surprise. "No. Or at least, I don't
think so."

"Do you consider Martina a friend?"

Doyle raised her brows at the question. "I'm afraid she's
past savin', Dr. Harding. She's goin' to wind up doin' hard
time—although mayhap I can go visit her, once she gets
herself sentenced."

He raised a skeptical brow. "Maghaberry Prison is quite a
distance away."

"Oh—no, she'll not likely go to Maghaberry. I keep makin'
that mistake, and mixin' it up."

"How is your hand?"

Dutifully, Doyle held it before her, flexing her fingers as
she had done with Acton in the car. "It seems much better—I
hardly think about it, bein' as I'm too busy tryin' to decide
why I'm being sent to various crime scenes so as to make a
flippin' fool of myself."

He tilted his head in mild disagreement. "Not so foolish,
perhaps; oftentimes the treatment for a somatic injury is to
attempt to pull the roots of the injury from the subconscious
to the conscious."

She stared at him for a long moment, and then slowly
shook her head. "Not a clue, what you just said."

"No matter," he replied. "Please continue."

With a frown, she tried to remember what they'd been
discussing. "My hand's much better, and in any event, I'll not
be goin' to the trainer anymore—Acton put the kibosh on it.

He worries overmuch, and doesn't like it when I slip the leash, and sneak off somewhere without Trenton."

Dr. Harding crossed his arms. "Ah yes; a classic love-triangle. A variation, perhaps, but stemming from the same impulses."

Doyle blinked in surprise. "I'm not truly havin' an affair with the trainer, Dr. Harding; I was just teasin' Acton."

"Oh, no; not you—you are very loyal. A classic allegiance-identifier."

At sea, she ventured, "Then who's in a love-triangle?"

But she was not to receive an answer, because she was suddenly awakened by Acton's attempt to carefully withdraw his arm from beneath her head. "Sorry," he said, and kissed her forehead. "Try to go back to sleep."

"No—I'm thoroughly awake, and ready for lunch."

Rubbing her eyes with her palms, Doyle sat up, and then heard the sound of familiar little footsteps, running pell-mell down the hallway. A voice called out, "Mum?" before small fingers could be observed, wiggling beneath the locked door.

"Edward," scolded Callie in hushed tones from the other side of the door. "No, no!"

"I'm comin, Edward—give me half a mo," Doyle called out to her son, and then turned to share a smile with Acton, who lay on the jumbled bed with an elbow bent beneath his head. "We've been twigged-out, husband."

"It would seem so."

They'd sneaked into the master suite by the downstairs entry, but Doyle had long ago come to the resigned conclusion that any such maneuverings were not going to escape the attention of Reynolds, and certainly not the building's security people. The lack of privacy was the price one paid for all the helpers who were underfoot, although the aforementioned helpers hadn't exactly covered themselves in glory, when they'd mistakenly allowed the villains in, on that memorable occasion.

Wincing at the memory, she tucked her hand beneath the opposite arm and firmly changed her train of thought by pausing for a moment to admire her husband. "Faith, you're a sight, Michael. Make sure to put on a shirt before you come out; we don't want Callie to be distracted from her pursuit of McGonigal."

"Not at all to my taste," he replied, unmoved.

"Well, I have it on good authority that men have a switch that switches on at the drop of a hat."

"Not mine," he maintained.

In heartfelt appreciation, she lay on his chest to kiss him. "One less worry, then. Should I tell Reynolds that you'll be joinin' us for lunch?"

"If you would, he said, as he ran his fingers through the fall of her hair. I cannot stay very long, unfortunately."

"New homicide?" she asked, half-hopefully. It had not escaped her attention that her assignments were few and far between, just now, which was only to be expected when her supervisor quailed before the mighty Chief Inspector Acton, and the mighty Chief Inspector Acton wanted to wrap his wife in cotton-wool.

Although on second thought, that wasn't exactly fair; Habib might quail before his commanding officer, but he'd had shown his mettle once before, back in Dublin, of all places; in a case that had featured its own Middle Eastern weapon. Which was the second time she'd thought of it, recently, even though there seemed no reason—that murder weapon certainly wasn't the same as the sword from the pawn shop—no question about that. No similarities at all, between that homicide and the charge-nurse's murder—not to mention that the motivation was completely different. The Dublin case was a retribution murder, plain and simple, and this one was an unsound-mind. Although plenty of people would argue that to commit a retribution murder, having an unsound-mind was something of a prerequisite—

Acton's voice interrupted her thoughts. "I must go meet with the Crown Court Commissioner; an unfortunate connection to a pending case has been uncovered, and it will require some careful handling."

This was interesting, and hinted at a political problem for the Met—corruption, or some high-up official getting caught doing something they oughtn't. With a smile, she shrugged her shoulders in mock-resignation. "Can't assign me, then; I'm not one who's good at careful handlin'."

"I might disagree," he said with a great deal of meaning.

She laughed, and decided this required yet another lingering kiss which turned into a series of lingering kisses, with Doyle wishing she hadn't promised Edward she'd be right up.

"Enough," she said, pulling away. "We need to eat, and Callie will be scandalized."

"You may shower first, then, and I will come up to join you."

After she'd dressed and set herself to rights, Doyle frowned in concentration as she walked past the stairway to the far end of the hall, so as to take the lift. There's another thing that's biting at me, she acknowledged; why would that nasty knife-murder in Dublin keep coming to mind? That's water so far under the bridge that it's out to the far isles, already.

With some exasperation, she ignored the persistent prickling of her scalp and paused before the lift. Honestly, what was the point of getting signals when she'd no clue what they meant? It was the same as the last time—what was that one about? Oh, right; it was when she'd been thinking about how the various women who'd made a run at Acton oftentimes wound up dead, for their sins, with Tim's sister Caroline at the head of the queue. Although—although Acton himself killed Caroline, and Martina killed the office manager, so she may be misunderstanding whatever it was she was supposed to be understanding, here. Or else she'd got her wires crossed; it happened, sometimes. Dr. Harding wanted her to be patient, which was all kinds of ironic because she wasn't a patient person—not at all. Instead, she was a leaper-to-conclusions, although there'd not been much leaping lately; instead it felt as though she'd been lurching about, with little to show for it.

Not true, she corrected herself immediately. Her hand was feeling better, and Acton was that relieved that she was behaving more like her old self—she could feel it. And today he wasn't day-drinking before noon, thank God fasting.

Doyle realized that she hadn't yet called the lift, and so she hurriedly touched the button. All in all, the situation was improving, mainly because she'd finally come to the realization that her husband was fast-descending into a black mood—drinking and brooding—and that such a turn of events was to be avoided at all costs. He tended to go scorched-earth, in his black moods, and it was a fearsome sight to behold, with little for her to do save hang on to his coat-tails, and try to pull him back from the brink. She hadn't been paying attention as she ought—and the black moods had been fewer and further between, lately—but shame on her, for not seeing that Acton needed a bit of help, in fending off his demons. There was no question he'd demons, had Acton.

Silently, the lift's doors opened, and she stepped within.

CHAPTER 21

$\mathcal{D}$oyle emerged into the kitchen, where Reynolds was carefully arranging the food on the plates—Reynolds always felt food presentation was important, which was probably something they taught you in butler-school, and it was a shame he didn't have a more appreciative audience.

Doyle announced, "Acton will have lunch, but he's in a bit of a hurry, so here's a heads-up."

"Very good madam."

Doyle kissed Edward and took her seat, duly noting that beneath his impassive expression, Reynolds was quite pleased. Pleased and—relieved, mayhap? He'd no doubt noticed that the master of the house was drinking deep, lately, and he probably knew as well as Doyle that a hearty bout of sex tended to head off said master's occasional black moods. Faith, it was a wonder the servant hadn't put on romantic music, and pushed them both through the bedroom door.

Her thoughts were interrupted when Acton himself appeared at the head of the stairs, and greeted them as he settled into his usual chair. As Reynolds promptly served his meal, he accepted a pasta noodle from his giggling son, and said to Doyle, "I am wondering if the wood stairs are too dangerous for Edward, since he'll be able to climb over the safety gate, soon. Perhaps it would be safer to carpet them."

Doyle could feel her cheeks flush hot, as she stammered, "Oh—oh, I suppose. Although he does likes to ride in the lift— he likes to push the buttons."

"Nevertheless, it poses a danger. Think about it, is all," he replied, and then said no more, as he began his meal.

He's noticed, she thought in acute dismay, and I'm that embarrassed that I'm being such a baby. She'd been avoiding the stairs, since it was on the stairs that she'd had the knock-down, drag-out battle with the evil Mr. Javid, who was now dead, and not a moment too soon, although she probably should pray for his sorry, sorry soul.

Acton interrupted her thoughts. "I heard from my mother, this morning."

Happy to assist in his change of subject, she gave him a look. "Katy, bar the door; what's she want?"

"She requested funds for the purpose of buying Father Clarence a vehicle. He travels quite a bit, since he is the only RC priest in the region, and she claims his own vehicle is very unreliable."

Doyle set down her fork to stare at him in astonishment. "Holy Mother, Michael. What's got into her?" The Dowager Lady Acton was not exactly known for her generous nature, not to mention she very much looked down upon anyone of the papist religion, her daughter-in-law first amongst them.

Acton shrugged slightly. "She must enjoy his company. Hudson seems to think he is harmless."

"Does he? That's good, I suppose—he's very long-headed, is Hudson. But it does give one pause—your mother's not easy company to keep. On the other hand, he's probably well-fed, when he's visitin', and I can assure you that country priests are always on the lookout for a good meal."

Acton offered Edward a bite of his own meal, and shot her an amused glance. "Apparently, she has him working on her memoirs."

Doyle had to laugh aloud, because the Dowager was just the sort of puffed-up person who would think that the world was clamoring to read her memoirs. "If it keeps her occupied, more power to her. Only don't let her give away any state secrets." This was a valid concern, as the House of Acton was steeped in secrets, many of them the type of secret that could not withstand the light of day.

"More likely it is but a ploy, to keep her visitor coming."

Doyle could only agree, "Aye; I imagine you have the right of it. Should we feel a bit sorry for her?"

"No," he replied without the slightest hesitation. Acton wasn't fond of his mother, and small blame to him; she'd plotted against him in the past, often with the willing assistance of Acton's cousin, Sir Stephen, who'd been hoping to inherit his title and Trestles.

Thus reminded, she said, "I wonder what Sir Stephen thinks about this visitin' priest wrinkle. He can't be happy with someone else havin' any influence over your mother."

"My mother tells me that Sir Stephen is very unhappy, because he believes he was being used by Lady Abby so as to allow her access to Howard."

Doyle could only agree with this assessment. "Knowin'

what we now know, that only makes sense, I suppose. It must be very lowerin' for him, to feel used in such a way."

Acton glanced up at her in amusement. "Please don't feel sorry for him, either."

She reasoned, "I know your relatives are a passel of blacklegs, Michael, but we're supposed to pray for their redemption, and give them every opportunity. People do come around, and try to mend themselves." As an excellent case in point, Doyle need look no further than Dr. Harding, who'd tried to kill her—once upon a time—and was now haunting her dreams and giving advice, for reasons unknown.

Her husband paused to meet her eyes with all seriousness. "You may pray as you wish, but you must never trust them, Kathleen. If I may say so, you are sometimes a bit naïve."

Rather than argue with this irrefutable fact, she shrugged a shoulder in concession. "Mayhap. Especially for someone who's in the business we're in."

"Indeed," he agreed. "It does tend to temper one's faith in mankind."

And since this topic was one she'd been angling to bring up, she quickly seized upon the opportunity presented. "Well, speakin' of such, unless you want me to start workin' on your memoirs, I'll need an assignment, husband. And that's a threat, by the by; your memoirs would not be for the faint of heart."

He checked the time, and folded his napkin to place it on the table. "I must go meet with the Crown Court Commissioner, but if you will see Miss Chaudhry, I will arrange for an assignment by the time you get there."

"Grand—thank you, Michael. But nothin' paltry," she warned.

"Certainly not," he said, and it wasn't exactly the truth

Doyle retrieved Edward's napkin from the floor. "What's to-do with the Crown Court Commissioner?"

"The delicate matter," he explained. "I am afraid I am not free to discuss it."

"Due to its bein' delicate," she teased. "Just be sure to make a note, so we'll have it for your memoirs."

"Best not," he replied, and kissed her goodbye.

CHAPTER 22

*E*verything's biting at me, Doyle acknowledged a bit crossly; and I'm that sick of being bit. I should have run away to hide under the bed when stupid Acton proposed stupid marriage, and I would have, if only he weren't so darkly handsome.

She was making her way up to Acton's office so as to receive her next assignment. It was a given that Acton wasn't going to allow his pregnant and semi-disabled wife to work on something juicy, like the charge-nurse murder, but hopefully it would be something halfway interesting, so that she could lord it over Munoz, who'd her own juicy murder. Although to be fair, that one was a quick roll-up, with Martina-the-murderess leaving a wide trail of breadcrumbs, just like an unsound-mind tended to do. But in any event, the fair Doyle wanted something new to work on, mainly became she needed a distraction from her thoughts, which were scattered, and rather ominous.

She frowned slightly, as walked across the bridge that

connected the two buildings. It was very unlike her, to feel so down-pin. It was coming on Christmas, after all, and since they'd successfully navigated some very rough weather this year, she should be rejoicing along with the season. Although it was true that Christmas made her miss her mother more than usual—just as she'd told Dr. Harding.

And speaking of which, it didn't help her general mood that she'd a ghost that was saying cryptic things—although the ghosts always did, and so it shouldn't be a wonder. Interesting, that it was Dr. Harding, yet again. Usually the ghosts had some sort of connection to whatever-it-was that Doyle was supposed to be figuring out, but in this case, she was stumped. Why had Dr. Harding come back to haunt her? When you thought about it, he was an unlikely ghost in the first place, since he'd once tried his level best to put a period to the fair Doyle. He and Caroline, Timothy McGonigal's sister—she'd given it a good try, too. Although the wretched Mr. Javid came in a close third, what with the recent life-or-death battle on the stairway at the flat.

Wincing, she turned her thoughts away from the morbid subject of people who'd tried to kill her, and instead pondered the ghost's message. Dr. Harding seemed to be hinting that she and Acton each had an unsound-mind, although she'd argued with him about it; her perceptive abilities were a gift from God, and she never truly resented them. Faith, they were a boon, in her quest to catch Acton before he did something truly terrible–although she didn't always manage it. For instance, there was that time—terrible indeed–when he'd killed Caroline McGonigal before her very eyes. Now, there was the trigger for a black mood like no other; Acton in vengeance-mode was a fearsome thing to behold.

Doyle shut her eyes briefly, and reminded herself that she was supposed to be trying to direct her thoughts away from morbid subjects—for the love o' Mike—and to stop circling back to Caroline and the various other worthies who'd done her harm. Although with Dr. Harding himself front and center, she could hardly be blamed.

She cast off these disquieting thoughts as she approached Nazy, who looked up from her desk with a shy smile. "Officer Doyle; I am expecting you."

"I'm beggin' for a case, Nazy, like a gypsy on the byway. Tell me you've a homicide for me."

"I do," the girl agreed, and handed Doyle a case-file. "Officer Gabriel is the Case Management Officer, and it is to him you will report."

Doyle eyed her suspiciously. "It's not the stupid burglary at the pawn shop, is it?"

"No, ma'am; it is a homicide. A Jane Doe, taken from the river."

"Almost as bad," Doyle pronounced. "Sorry, Nazy; I don't mean to sound ungrateful, but I have to keep up with Munoz, or the next thing you know, she'll be promoted and I'll be takin' orders from her."

Nazy looked a bit conscious, as she leaned forward slightly and lowered her voice. "Isn't Officer Munoz in trouble?"

Doyle blinked. "Munoz is in trouble?"

Her eyes wide, Nazy quickly backpedaled. "Oh—oh, I shouldn't have said."

"Oh, yes, you should," Doyle assured her. "I swear on all the holy relics I won't say you told me."

Nazy took a quick, covert glance down the hall. "I shouldn't say, because I don't really know, but I wondered why the Chief Inspector wanted to meet with her, the other day." Again, she lowered her voice. "I thought perhaps she was being reprimanded—they seemed very serious."

"Haven't heard a whisper," Doyle confessed. This was not surprising, actually, since Acton tended to be very careful about keeping personnel matters from her. And with good reason, of course; only see how she was winkling information from Nazy, who tended to be a ripe target for information-winkling.

Thinking over this nugget of information, however, Doyle ventured, "It seems unlikely Acton would be doing the reprimanding for a DS, though; usually that's the direct supervisor's job."

"I may be mistaken," Nazy agreed, but Doyle could see that she didn't think so. It was all very interesting–that Munoz would be haled before Acton for a dressing-down, and it would probably behoove the fair Doyle to find out what had gone down, if for no other reason than crass curiosity.

Reminded, she asked, "Did you hear how the taking-into-custody went, for Martina Betancourt? I bet Sir Vikili, was fit to be tied." This in a teasing tone, because Nazy carried a mighty torch for the famous solicitor.

Nazy nodded, her dark eyes alight. "I heard it went without incident, and that she was transferred to Wexton Prison, until the preliminary hearing." With palpable disappointment, she added, "And the Chief Inspector was set to meet with Sir Vikili about the evidence disclosure schedule this afternoon, but the Chief Inspector cancelled the meeting."

"Oh—right; somethin' else has come up, and he's been

called over by the Crown Court Commissioner to huddle-up. Any idea what that's all about?"

Nazy shook her head. "No, ma'am. It is not on his calendar."

It was now Doyle's turn to backpedal, and so she offered, "Forget I said anythin', then. We'll have our mutual secrets, and take a blood-oath."

Nazy laughed, and Doyle added, "Speakin' of which, I hear that Officer Gabriel is seein' your friend in Personnel."

With a conspiratorial smile, Nazy nodded. "Yes—Marjan. Only she's no longer in Personnel, she's been transferred to the Crown Court Liaison Services."

Doyle arched a brow. "She has? Gabriel had best look lively, then; she'll be seeing Sir Vikili on a regular basis, over there."

"Marjan doesn't see Sir Vikili more than I do," Nazy protested. "And anyway, she has a boyfriend, now."

"There you go. You've got the inside track, in the Sir Vikili stakes."

The girl sighed. "He is *so* handsome."

"You'd have beautiful children together."

Nazy giggled, and Doyle didn't have the heart to burst this air-dream by informing her that Sir Vikili was irrevocably in love with his sister-in-law, and unlikely to fall victim to anyone else's lures. And—in an interesting turn of events— said sister-in-law was now a widow, thanks to Mr. Javid's untimely death on the Acton stairway.

With a mighty effort, Doyle reminded herself that she was not going to keep dwelling on it, and instead firmly launched onto a different subject. "Well, when you finally land Sir Vikili, he can hang your weddin' portrait in the place of that other paintin' about the forbidden lovers—whatever their names were."

"Vis and Ramin," Nazy supplied.

"Right; that's the one." Frowning slightly, Doyle ventured, "Tell me, Nazy—about those forbidden lovers–"

"Yes?"

Almost afraid to hear the answer, Doyle nevertheless continued, "What happens—in the story, I mean? Is it one of those miserable Greek stories, where everyone dies in the end?"

Nazy lifted her brows in surprise. "Oh no, Officer Doyle—instead, they finally marry, and live long and happy lives together."

For a long moment, Doyle stared at her. "Do they indeed? Well, the Persians should explain to the Greeks how stories are supposed to go."

"I'm not sure the Greeks would appreciate it," Nazy offered doubtfully.

Doyle nodded, and straightened up. "Right. Best not stir-up more trouble than there already is. And speakin' of which, I'm off to see Officer Gabriel, to help him solve his paltry Jane Doe."

"Good luck, ma'am," Nazy called after her.

CHAPTER 23

*A*s it turned out, when Doyle called Gabriel to ask if he was available, he was downstairs in the lobby, on his way to take a drive over to the appropriate Borough's morgue. "I'll wait for you, Sergeant, and you can ride along. You can think of things I should ask the coroner."

Doyle made a wry mouth, because Gabriel was unlikely to need any help in that department. "Grand; I'll meet you at the garage in two shakes."

She texted Acton, not expecting him to pick up, but he did, his voice quiet. "Yes?"

"I'm going along with Gabriel to take a look at his Jane Doe, just so you know I'm not gettin' shipped over to the morgue as a corpse."

"Good thought. I would have wondered."

She smiled into the phone. "How's it goin'?" she asked, hoping to get a hint of whatever-it-was he was there for, that even Nazy didn't know about. Hopefully it was not yet another crooked-judges scandal; faith, they'd have to start recruiting judges from straight off the street, if this kept up.

"It is going well," he replied quietly, and this was true.

So; she was not to glean any hints, which was probably just as well–what the man handled day-to-day would probably make her hair turn grey, "I'll check in later–cheers," she said, and rang off.

She found Gabriel waiting at the unmarked vehicle in the parking garage, and they exchanged greetings as they got into the car, and were underway.

As he pulled into traffic, he remarked, "This reminds me of old times at the racecourse, Sergeant."

Doyle pointed out, "We never did make it to the racecourse, thank God fastin'."

"You're right; I stand corrected. And it's probably not a coincidence that I'm under strict instructions to keep you out of trouble."

She smiled at this reference to Acton, which he was probably not supposed to say, but one of the reasons she liked Gabriel is that he tended to say whatever he wished. "Faith; I don't look for trouble. Instead, trouble looks for me, and I'm pig-sick of bein' so easily found out, believe me."

"Well then; this may not be an auspicious start, because I wanted to ask you something, off the record."

She looked over at him with all curiosity. "Ask away."

"What do you know about Philippe Savoie?"

Doyle was reminded that Gabriel had been asking the clerk at the pawn shop about a man with a scar on his face, and drew the obvious conclusion. After deciding that she could be just as plain-spoken as her companion, she replied, "D'you mean aside from his latest adventures in petty theft?"

He smiled slightly, at being caught out. "Not so petty, as it turns out."

Quickly, Doyle tried to sort through what she should and should not say, which seemed to be the usual state of affairs when she was dealing with her husband's doings. "I know Savoie's a slippery one, but I also know that he runs by his own code, in a strange way."

"Do you think he's capable of murder?"

Definitely, thought Doyle, who'd been a front-row witness, and on more than one occasion. But aloud, she asked, "Why? D'you think he's killed this Jane Doe?"

"No—no," he said immediately, and it was the truth. Slowly, he added, "But there are times I have the feeling that I'm being led."

Diplomatically, Doyle made no comment, because there'd been many a time that she'd felt she was being led, herself, only in her case she was always being led away. Her wedded husband was a past master at distracting the fair Doyle from his aforesaid doings.

And because the last thing she wanted to tell Gabriel was that Savoie robbed the pawn shop because Acton wanted his stupid necklace back, she asked in all innocence, "How so?"

He shrugged. "It may be my imagination. And I'm thinking that it may behoove me not to look for any more trouble, right now."

This desire resonated with her, and she nodded in sympathy, as she gazed out at the scenery. "You do get gun-shy, after trouble's bit you a few times."

"Not you," he countered. "You charge in like the Light Brigade."

She made a wry mouth, not at all clear on the reference, but understanding the intent. "You'd be surprised, my friend. I'm ready to take a good, long break from perp-struggles."

"Me, too, and I've a bullet-hole to show for it."

Thus reminded, she asked, "Is Munoz still on probation for her DOD?" As a result of the same case where Gabriel had been shot, Munoz had been reprimanded for dereliction of duty, and it suddenly occurred to Doyle that this could have been the reason for the mysterious Acton-and-Munoz meeting.

"No," he replied. "She's too smart to get into any real trouble, which was why we broke up."

This seemed to be a reference to his drug addiction, and so Doyle offered with all due sympathy, "A lesson learned, my friend."

"The hard way," he agreed. "It came from having too much money for my own good."

"Well, money's the root of all evil," Doyle noted. "We definitely see it, in this business—a lot of murders are for material gain."

"Money and love, I think, are the main movers."

But Doyle shook her head. "You don't murder out of love, Gabriel; not *real* love, leastways. It's always thwarted-love, instead. Real love *"bears all things, believes all things, hopes all things, and endures all things."*

"Again, I stand corrected," he said. "This is a very edifying car ride."

She smiled, and turned to face him. "Love is supposed to be generous, too. You could spend your money on charitable causes–there must be some that you admire."

He lifted his shoulders slightly. "I'm not much for charitable causes, but I could start collecting something. I could try to emulate Sir Vikili's collections; art, and ancient weapons."

Doyle offered, "He collects jewelry too, I think."

"Now, that's much more my style."

He lapsed into silence and Doyle had the sense he was deep in thought. She ventured "Should we talk about the case?"

His dark brows raised, he glanced over at her. "Are you leading me off-topic?"

She laughed. "Faith no; I'm not smart enough. Instead, I'm the one who's always gettin' steered off-topic like a dog sent off to fetch a stick. I don't know as I can tell you anythin' of interest about Savoie, and I may not be inclined to, anyways. He did me a massive favor, once upon a time, and so while I'll not shield him, I'll not go out of my way to attack him, either."

He nodded. "Fair enough–I'll not pry, then. I suppose we can always speak of this case, as a last resort."

"I haven't yet read the report," she confessed.

"No real need–it seems fairly straightforward, but the Borough's coroner wanted us to have a look, because a few things don't add up."

Doyle perked up, because this was of interest; unfortunately, unidentified bodies were fished out of the Thames on a regular basis, and the CID tended to waste little time or effort on any which were unclaimed. If no one was frantically wondering where their loved-one was, the decedent was unlikely to be anything other than a burn-out— either taking her own life, or having a misadventure that had killed her, usually one connected to alcohol or drugs. The few times the CID did get interested was when the Doe looked to be the victim of an unsound-mind, which then raised the possibility of a serial killer.

"Do they think it was an unsound-mind?" she prompted.

"No—she drowned, and sometime in the early morning hours, judging from the state of the corpse. However, the coroner's office is surprised that no one has filed a missing-persons report; the body's well-tended, and they say she's given birth, sometime within the past year."

Doyle nodded. "Then that does seem odd—that no one's missin' her. She may have been long-hauled here, for a body-dump."

"That's what I'm thinking, and if that's the case, then we've got ourselves a homicide. If no inquiries are made after a few days, we might post-up a "can you identify" in the media. If we send it wide, someone must know who she is."

"Nothin' on CCTV?"

He shook his head. "They can estimate where she entered the river, based on tide and current, but they can't get it exact, especially in this central London area, where the currents are so ferocious. Unfortunately, that means a lot of CCTV tape to review—and who knows if there's anything to see in the first place."

"Slog work," Doyle pronounced. "No wonder I was recruited."

He laughed. "Now, Sergeant, chin up; we'll see what the coroner's people have to say, first. Maybe the killer pinned a note to her chest."

"That would be just my luck," Doyle groused. "Yet another case to be rolled-up within the hour."

CHAPTER 24

*T*he Borough's coroner pulled out the body-drawer in the cold morgue, and then began to carefully unzip the body bag—Doyle always felt it was the sign of a good coroner when they treated the decedent's remains with respect; everyone deserved human dignity, even burn-outs who'd wound up unclaimed, on a grim, cold slab in the local morgue.

As the pale, still face was revealed, however, Doyle exclaimed in astonishment, "Oh; oh—I know her. She's— she's Lady Abby; Lady Abby-something. Holy *Mother*."

The coroner looked up in surprise. "She's an aristo? They couldn't come up with a Missing Persons match, and her prints have eroded."

Doyle closed her eyes with the effort to remember what she knew. "She's from somewhere up north—Rosings, or Hunsford, or something. I forget, but she's been staying here in town, lately. Faith, I'd best call Acton." She paused, and belatedly remembered the protocols. "If that's all right with you, Officer Gabriel."

"By all means," said Gabriel. "It's not every day you fish an 'honorable' out of the river."

Not exactly honorable, thought Doyle as she scrolled for her husband's work number. And poor Mary; more trouble to be brought to her door. It didn't take a genius to figure out that Lady Abby hadn't much liked being on the receiving end of a dressing-down by Howard, and must have promptly thrown her sorry self into the river as a final, spiteful act.

Her message went straight to Acton's voice-mail, and so Doyle told him, "Somethin's come up—it's not a t-call, but give me a ring when you've a chance."

"What can you tell us?" Gabriel asked the coroner.

The woman reviewed her notes. "She was spotted by a fisherman, because her clothing was caught on a piling down the river from Tower Bridge." She then glanced over at Doyle with a small smile. "Not Greyfriars Bridge, you'll be happy to hear, Officer Doyle."

"I am, that," Doyle replied with her pinned-on smile, and wished everyone would just let the stupid bridge-jumping incident *go*, for the *love* o' Mike.

"No penetration wounds?" asked Gabriel.

This seemed an odd question to Doyle; if the decedent had a stab wound, they'd have heard about it by now.

"No." the woman shook her head. "But I did wonder if the death may have been inflicted by a second party, because there's traces of subcutaneous bruising, on the back of her head." She leaned forward, and shifted the corpse carefully. "It's hard to see, due to the discoloration, and it's also possible that the bruising may have happened when her hair caught on debris in the river. Do you see, here? But it does raise the possibility that she was held down, in the water."

The two detectives leaned down to scrutinize the indicated area. "Alcohol or drugs involved?" asked Gabriel.

"Nothing evident, but I can call for a screen—we didn't see the need, as yet."

"Let's do it, please."

"Interestin', that no one's missin' her," Doyle mused. "She has a family in wherever-it-is, I'm fairly certain. Mayhap she doesn't check-in very often."

"And there's the baby, too," the coroner noted.

Doyle raised her head to stare at her. "What baby?"

With a nod of her head, the coroner indicted the corpse. "The autopsy showed she's had a baby within the past year, so you'd think someone would know that she hasn't come home, even if it's just the babysitter. Unless she gave the baby up for adoption, or it didn't survive."

"Holy *Mother*," Doyle breathed yet again.

Gabriel cocked his head. "What?"

With a mighty effort to gather her wits about her, Doyle replied, "I'll tell you in a minute, but in the meantime let's put everything on hold until DCI Acton takes a look."

"Yes ma'am," the woman said, in the wooden tone of one who realizes this was no ordinary corpse, who'd managed to get herself drowned in the River Thames.

"If that's all right with you, sir," Doyle hurriedly asked Gabriel, who was supposed to be the lead officer.

"I concur. Let's step outside." He nodded to the coroner. "Thank you."

He followed Doyle down the fluorescent-lighted hallway, and Doyle offered over her shoulder, "Should we go outside, mayhap?" She gave him a look, because they'd shared an experience once, about being overheard in a room that was not as secure as it had first seemed.

"Certainly. It is a lovely day." This, because it was cold, and coming down buckets.

Once outside, they huddled under a nearby door arch, with Doyle thrusting her hands in her pockets only to discover that her pockets contained gloves—new gloves that she hadn't put there. As she pulled them on, she explained, "Sorry to be so mysterious, Gabriel, but it's a rare tangle-patch—in fact, it's that thwarted-love thing, rearing its ugly head again. Lady Abby was engaged to Nigel Howard, who's an MP and who is now my nanny's husband. The decedent has been—well, she'd been pestering them lately, and acting a bit hysterical."

"Ah."

Although it hardly seemed necessary, Doyle added, "If the baby's his, it would be a massive scandal."

He bowed his head in acknowledgement. "Even worse, if she was murdered."

Agape, Doyle stared at him. "Oh—I hadn't got that far. D'you truly think she was?"

"The jury's out, for the time being, but it's a possibility." He tilted his head toward her. "How friendly is Mr. Howard with your husband?"

Doyle drew her brows together. "That doesn't matter, Gabriel," she replied hotly. "Murder is murder."

Gabriel took a casual glance down the street. "Why are we waiting for the Chief Inspector, then?"

"Because he'll know how best to handle it." Her tone was a bit short, because she was nettled by the implication in the questions. "The decedent's a nob, Howard's an MP, and so it's a PR situation, which is when the brass *always* calls-in

Acton."

"Sorry," he said immediately. "I didn't mean to imply anything untoward."

This was untrue, and so Doyle forced herself to climb down from her high horse and acknowledge that the man had a point. "No, I'm sorry, too—I shouldn't have jumped on you. Mainly, I imagine Acton's not going to be happy that this little discovery might draw-in our poor nanny—we're very fond of her."

"Yes, I remember; wasn't Williams keen on her for a while?"

Doyle quirked her mouth. "Everyone's been keen on her, my friend—she's a walkin' angel. I'll admit that at the time, I was hopin' she'd wind up with Williams, because it would have been a nice change—he tended to fall victim to schemin' trollops."

"Speaking on behalf of all men, I will defend Williams, and point out that we all do—we can't seem to help it."

She chuckled, even as she pulled her coat tighter around her. "Faith; you sound like Williams—that's exactly what he said. But we're goin' off-topic, as usual."

He raised his brows. "But are we? Lady Abby sounds like she was a level-six scheming trollop."

The reference was to the police code that allowed for maximum restraint on a suspect, and Doyle had to smile. "Well, whichever level her sins, we owe her an investigation."

He nodded, and glanced up the rainy, deserted street. "Right. Whether the findings will be made public is another matter."

"I suppose," Doyle reluctantly agreed, and then sighed. "All right—let's go back in; I'm freezin'."

CHAPTER 25

*C*cton appeared within the hour, and listened to Gabriel's report as Doyle held up her gloved hands behind Gabriel's back and mouthed, "Thank you."

"Let's take a look," said Acton, and they withdrew back into the morgue, where the coroner gave him a respectful summary; it wasn't every day she worked on a nob, and it definitely wasn't every day that Chief Inspector Acton listened to her report.

His first question, however, was not what Doyle was expecting. "Who called you in?"

"The Thames Marine Unit," she replied. "A fisherman saw her, and alerted the marine police."

"But they did not consider hers a suspicious death?"

"No sir. They checked her against the Missing Persons Register, didn't find any 'possibles,' and so gave her over for a summary autopsy."

Acton nodded thoughtfully as he scrutinized the corpse. "She was alive when she went in?"

"Yes, sir—death by asphyxiation; water in the lungs. There are traces of algae in the liver and kidneys."

"It was too late to get prints?"

"Yes, sir." Bodies tended to decompose in the river fairly quickly.

"Have you bagged her clothes?"

"Yes sir; let me call for them."

As she did, Acton bent down to take a long, careful look at the subcutaneous bruising that the coroner had pointed out.

"What are you thinkin', sir?" Doyle asked into the silence. It seemed clear that something had caught his attention.

He straightened up, and replied, "If it is indeed a homicide, is of interest that she was so easily found."

This was actually a good point; if there were dark doings at play, surely the body would have been weighted down, or thrown further out to sea, instead of near Tower Bridge where there was a very good chance it would be discovered fairly quickly. A lot of people drowned in that area of the Thames every year, which was one of the reasons the Marine Unit had a dock on site.

Doyle ventured, "We were wonderin' if mayhap it was a body-dump, and she died elsewhere, but that doesn't seem plausible."

"No; I think not."

The coroner offered, "I think that's why we first assumed it was death by misadventure, sir; it doesn't appear there was any attempt made to obscure time and cause of death." She nodded in the direction of the corpse. "Save for the bruising on her head, but that seems a slender thread, to open an inquest."

Acton looked up at her. "Do you have a sense, either way?"

Slowly, the coroner shook her head. "No, sir."

The tagged bag of clothes was brought in, and Acton donned gloves so as to carefully examine them on the steel table. "Time of death?" he asked.

"Approximately two in the morning. The water was near freezing, though, so we can't be precise—within two hours, perhaps."

They stood in silence, processing this information, and Gabriel offered, "Shall I interview the fisherman, and the marine officers, sir?"

"Please," said Acton. "And I will give you her family's information, if you would have them contacted by local police."

Gabriel nodded. "Are the family potential suspects? Should I send a detective team to question them?"

"Not as yet," Acton said. "I believe she was estranged from her family."

"I wonder where the baby is, then?" asked Doyle.

"The baby is with a caregiver in Shoreditch," Acton replied. "A little boy."

CHAPTER 26

"I'm that gobsmacked," Doyle exclaimed in wonder, as soon as she was alone in the car with Acton. "Small wonder that she's been pesterin' Howard, if there's a secret baby in the mix."

"Indeed," he agreed, but she could see that he was distracted, and deep in thought. They were driving back to headquarters, as Gabriel had been dispatched to interview his witnesses.

My husband wants me well-away from this, Doyle thought; he doesn't want me to hear if any lies are being told, until he figures out what to do with this mess. It seemed clear to her that he was genuinely surprised by this turn of events, and was thinking over what he was going to do.

She prompted, "And you knew all about the baby, you wretched man."

He shrugged a shoulder in apology. "Howard asked me to be discreet."

"Aye; you're a first-class sphinx," she agreed. "The keeper

of many secrets, and I suppose it was just as well, since I'm a first-class gabbler. Does Mary know?"

"No. Or at least, I do not believe so."

"Mother a' Mercy, Michael; d'you think Howard *killed* the wretched woman?" This, of course, was the hundred-pound question; if the working-theory was homicide, Howard would be the prime suspect.

Slowly, her husband replied, "I would be surprised, but I have been surprised before."

Doyle nodded in agreement with this assessment. "Aye; I wouldn't have pegged him as a killer, even though it does seem that he's changed quite a bit, from how he used to be—before he was a politician. I suppose it's hard to be filled with righteous principles when your day-to-day life is necessarily filled with compromises, and horse-tradin'. If he wants to make a difference, he's probably got to go along with a lot of things he'd rather not."

"If he wishes to advance in that environment, he must undoubtedly make compromises," Acton agreed.

She heard a nuance, underlying his tone, and declared, "A bit scornful, you are, because you never compromise your principles with anyone, ever, but that's mainly because you're a nob, and see yourself as a superior being in the first place."

He smiled slightly. "You are harsh, Lady Acton."

"Don't start nobbin' back at me, my friend; I may have the title, but I'm not born-and-bred, like you are. You people think the rules don't apply to you, and speakin' of which, please don't tell me that you fell victim to wretched Lady Abby, too."

"Not at all to my taste," he replied with another smile, echoing what he'd said about Callie.

"No," she agreed. "Your type is a dim Irish shant, sportin' a wonky hand."

He lifted her hand to kiss its back. "Your hand seems to be improving."

"I can't help but notice that you did not dispute the 'dim' part of the description."

"Unfair," he replied. "I would never describe you as dim."

She smiled, as this was the pure truth, and he'd know she knew it. "Well, lately my little light has been dimmed a bit," she admitted. "It comes from this miserable weather, and havin' pregnant-brain, and tryin' to hide the aforementioned wonky hand from you."

"Should we go somewhere warm for a few weeks?" he asked. "Bermuda does sound inviting."

Doyle tried to imagine Acton sitting on the beach with a fruity rum drink, and came up empty. "No—it wouldn't seem like Christmas, Michael," she protested. "And there's even less chance that there'll be snow."

"A very good point."

She knit her brow. "You know, speakin' of which, Gabriel brought up somethin' with the coroner that didn't seem to be a good point—it was very unlike him."

"How so?"

Oh—oh, faith; there's that gabbling problem again, she realized, and wished she hadn't said anything. "I don't want to get him in trouble, Michael; he's had trouble enough."

"If he is relapsing, it is a serious matter, Kathleen."

She sighed in acknowledgement. "I know. I don't have that sense, though—I think he's learned a hard lesson, and has turned a leaf."

"What was the point you believe he missed?"

Naturally, Acton wasn't going to be distracted by her

assurances, and so she reluctantly revealed, "He asked the coroner if Lady Abby had any penetration wounds, which seemed a bit strange, since if she did, there wouldn't be any question that we were dealin' with a homicide."

Acton was silent for a moment. He then offered, "Gabriel's light has been dimmed lately, also."

"Aye, that," she acknowledged fairly.

"Please let me know if you notice if anything else unusual."

"I will," she agreed. "And little did you know that my sleeveless Jane Doe case was going to blow up in your face. What will we do about the Howard and Mary situation?"

"Let me think on it a bit."

She eyed him sidelong, and said with some emphasis, "If Howard's killed her, we have to go after him, Michael; no matter what."

"Agreed."

He lapsed into silence again, and Doyle gazed out the window, thinking over this latest catastrophe, and the effects it would have on her poor household—although she shouldn't be so selfish, and instead remember that there were other innocents who would suffer a more catastrophic loss. "How old's the baby? He can't be much of a baby—faith, he must be comin' on two years, by now. After all, Mary and Howard met at your confirmation reception."

Acton tilted his head. "I believe the child was conceived at a later date."

Yet again, Doyle turned to stare at him, agape. "Holy Mother; never say Howard was still dallyin' with Lady Abby *after* he'd met Mary? Faith, Michael, that's hard to believe—they were so in love."

"Only once, according to Howard. It was in Dublin, when

she'd pursued him there. He says he tried to placate her, and one thing led to another."

Thoroughly astonished, Doyle could only stare at him. "*What?*"

With a thread of amusement, he shrugged a shoulder. "I did not ask for the particulars."

In wonder, Doyle turned to gaze out the windscreen. "How could he have been so weak—she's so *obviously* a schemin' trollop. And more bad news for poor Mary, who is slated to have a truly terrible Christmas, especially if Howard's the prime suspect in a containment murder."

"It may be best to avoid all the unpleasantness, and spend the holidays at Trestles," he suggested. "It would have the added benefit of giving Mary some time and privacy, so as to work matters out with her husband."

Oh-oh, thought Doyle, as her dimmed wits suddenly stirred to life. Oh-oh.

Mustering up a casual tone, she smiled slightly. "I'll admit it's temptin', my friend."

He nodded. "Think on it—it may be best for all concerned. And I can arrange for snow to be brought in for Edward, if you'd like."

"Because of course, you can," she agreed. "You're the next thing to a magician." But she said it absently, because clarity had hit her poor muddled brain like a sudden bolt of lightning. Clarity, and a feeling of that deja view—or whatever the phrase was—that meant she'd been here, before. Rouse yourself, Doyle, she thought with grim determination; you're dim indeed, not to have seen what's been laid plainly before you.

CHAPTER 27

cton had left to go meet with Howard, and he'd suggested, rather apologetically, that the fair Doyle stay at headquarters until he returned, rather than go home for the afternoon as per her usual schedule. Lady Abby's death was something she couldn't not mention to those at home, and Acton wanted to speak to Howard, first.

"You don't want me to come along with you, and listen-in to what he has to say?" she asked a bit pointedly.

"I do, but he'd think it strange if you were present, given the circumstances."

This was a fair point—and it was the truth—and so she agreed to work on her report until he'd finished his meeting, and then returned to huddle with her. It was just as well—she needed to dust off her dimmed light, and figure out what the man was up to.

It was all rather symmetrical, actually, and it was one of the reasons she'd had her sudden jolt of clarity in the car—that sense that she'd been here, before. Acton wanted to go on holiday—Bermuda, of all places—but he'd settled on Trestles, which may as well be Bermuda in terms of being cut off from daily life. Acton was bound and determined to go on holiday, and the last time they'd gone on holiday—the only time, truly —was when they'd gone to Dublin, where—coincidentally— Lady Abby had first shown her true colors.

But, as it turned out, Acton hadn't wanted to go on holiday to Dublin as much as he'd wanted to get out of town because he was orchestrating a bit of bloody vengeance, and he didn't want the fair Doyle to catch on, as she'd a wont to do.

She'd been slow on the uptake, not to have seen this troubling sign, because Acton never wanted to set foot outside of his fortress, where he could control everything, just as he was controlling everything, now. She shut her eyes, trying to come up with the elusive thought that was just out of reach. What was he controlling? Lady Abby's murder, if it was indeed a murder? That didn't seem to be it; although her husband had known about the secret baby, Doyle knew—in the way that she knew things—that Acton was genuinely surprised by the woman's appearance in the local morgue.

"So, what's he up to?" she asked aloud.

"What's who up to?" asked Munoz, who leaned to cross her arms atop Doyle's cubicle wall.

"Nothin'," Doyle said crossly. "You shouldn't sneak-up like that, Munoz."

With supreme unconcern, Munoz sipped her coffee. "How's the hand?"

"It's none of your business," Doyle said hotly.

"I think we've already gone over this, Doyle."

With poor grace, Doyle conceded, "Aye. Sorry—I'm all

MURDER IN UNSOUND MIND

distracted, and such. My stupid hand is doin' much better, thank you."

"Good. What's up?"

My husband's plotting mayhem, Doyle thought, but aloud she said, "Have you spoken with Gabriel recently?"

"No. Not a good idea."

"Oh—oh, right. I just wanted to ask—" yet again, she realized that perhaps she was gabbling where she oughtn't, and paused.

With a sharp glance, the other girl lowered her coffee. "Is there something wrong with Gabriel?"

Doyle knew what she was implying, and so she replied, "I don't have the sense that he's relapsed, or anythin'. He just seems—well, he seems rather *grave*, for Gabriel. He's usually so devil-may-care."

Munoz considered this. "He's had a tough year."

"Aye, that—in spades."

"Do you think he needs help?"

Doyle lifted her chin to stare at her. "Mayhap. Faith, I'm not much of a friend, not to think to ask."

Munoz sipped her coffee. "It's hard to know whether or not to intrude, sometimes."

"Yes—I'll go talk to him. I should give him a case-status report, anyways."

"Don't mention me," Munoz warned, and then wandered away toward Habib's cubicle.

Thus prompted, Doyle texted Gabriel to ask if he was available for a status report once he was back from the witness interview, and whilst she awaited his reply, she raised her head to stare at her reflection in the blank computer screen. That's funny, she thought; just now—when I was speaking with Munoz—I'd the sense there was something beneath her words, when we were talking about Gabriel. Mayhap that's what she'd gone to Acton's office to talk about—she was worried about Gabriel, but couldn't very well speak to her ex-beau directly. It was the same old cleft-stick; police officers didn't want to admit to any failings, but those self-same failings may put others in danger. Munoz must have felt she'd no choice but to raise the matter with Acton, whom she knew would address it discreetly, and hopefully without getting Gabriel in any more hot water than he already was. After all, Acton was the keeper of secrets like no other.

Doyle frowned at her reflection, because despite this seemingly plausible explanation, she was left with the niggling feeling that this was not, in fact, the reason for the aforesaid meeting. I should try to winkle-out from Acton what it was that he and Munoz talked about, she thought; I have a feeling it would behoove me to find out.

Gabriel pinged to say he'd return soon, and he could meet her at his office. Happy for the excuse to abandon her report, Doyle decided that a half-cup of coffee wouldn't come amiss —she'd a very busy day, thus far—and so went to fetch some at the canteen, dawdling a bit so that she could check-in with Edward on the way.

"Here he is," said Callie. "Edward, here's your mum."

Edward issued a string of mostly unintelligible words whilst he happily displayed his dinosaur on the mobile screen, and Doyle kept up as best she could. After Callie had wrested the phone back from him, Doyle explained, "I'm hung-up, here at headquarters for a bit, so I'll probably miss the park-walk today."

"No worries, Lady Acton; I wasn't sure whether we were cleared to go, anyways."

"Oh; oh, that's right." Since Doyle wasn't at liberty to explain that the Lady Abby dragon had been well-and-thoroughly slain, she did not pass comment, but said instead, "If the weather's clear for two minutes together, feel free to enlist Trenton and go somewhere else—our best defense is to wear the boyo out. You could always drive over to St. Margaret's and let him run around with Emile and Gemma, when they get out from school."

"Yes, madam," said Callie in a carefully neutral tone. "That is a good idea."

This was not true, and as Doyle rang off, she thought, that's interesting; I forgot that I suspect Callie's avoiding Savoie for some reason, and it would probably behoove me to find out why. It's hard to believe Savoie made a pass at her—I don't think she's to his taste, as Acton would say. Mayhap it was Trenton, who was being too friendly? That seemed equally unlikely, since Trenton always kept himself to himself. It was not completely unthinkable for either of them, of course; Callie was a comely lass, and men had that man-switch, after all.

She paid for her coffee—a little more than a half-cup, since there was no sense in wasting this opportunity—and thought over this potential development as she wandered out the canteen doors. It might be rather sweet, if Trenton and Callie were to make a match of it—even though he was a bit older. He wasn't as old as McGonigal, of course, and Acton was practically casting the girl on a fishing lure in front of Tim. And then there was Adrian, the new driver, who seemed to have warm feelings for the girl, himself.

As she walked down the hall, impatiently waiting for her coffee to cool, she realized she was so busy matchmaking that she was missing the main point—Callie was uneasy about something, and Doyle should find out the cause—the poor girl should not be made uncomfortable, whether it was because she was the object of flirtation, or because she'd witnessed some Savoie-style menace.

Another mental note, she instructed herself; find out what Acton and Munoz talked about at their meeting, and find out what happened at the park that's made Callie wary of Savoie.

I should write it all down, she thought a bit distractedly; I've not been good at mental notes, lately.

CHAPTER 28

"Sergeant," Gabriel greeted her as he saw her waiting outside his office door. "What are you avoiding, that you're such an eager beaver?"

She followed him in, smiling at being thus caught out. "My report. I hate writin' reports, and any excuse to avoid it."

As he slung down his rucksack, he cocked his head. "Isn't the report for me?"

"Oh-oh," she replied. "Forget I said."

He settled into his chair, and opened his computer screen. "Well, I wish I could add to your report, but the discovering witness didn't have much to say."

With a small frown, Doyle leaned forward. "What d'you think about Acton's theory? That she was too easily found, if she was indeed murdered?"

"I think that's a good point, and why the Chief Inspector gets all the accolades."

Doyle took a guess at what "accolades" meant, and nodded thoughtfully. "It rather lends toward 'misadventure', then. If her old lover wanted to kill her because she'd shown up with a pesky baby, he'd have done a better job of hidin' the body."

Gabriel glanced up as he typed. "On the other hand, that may be exactly what the killer was hoping—that we'd think 'misadventure,' and close the book. After all, it was the merest luck that you were on the assignment, and recognized her."

Doyle held her tongue, because it had long been her experience that when such a thing happened, it truly wasn't luck at all, but was connected to some ghost-driven thing that she was supposed to be ferreting-out. In this instance, however, she was at a loss—Dr. Harding was the current ghost, and he didn't seem much interested in Lady Abby and her unsound-mind.

"What do you think?" Gabriel asked, giving her a speculative glance. "Is Howard someone who could have done this?"

Slowly, Doyle offered, "I'd say 'no,' but I haven't been spendin' much time with him, lately. I know he's very keen on advancin' in politics, though. His poor wife is a bit bewildered by it all."

Gabriel cocked his head. "We'll wait to hear from the Chief Inspector, then; maybe he has a confession already in hand."

She knew he was joking, but she shook her head, nonetheless. "I truly hope not, Gabriel. Mary's a friend, and this would bring down the whirlwind on her poor head." She paused, thinking about it. "And that whirlwind is atop the whirlwind that's already comin' down, even if Howard's not a suspect; she's goin' to find out about the baby, at the very least."

Gabriel shrugged. "Let this be a lesson to him not to dabble in adultery."

In Howard's defense, Doyle offered, "Well, he wasn't married to Mary at the time, so I don't think it qualifies as 'adultery,' exactly, but it will nonetheless be a heavy blow, poor thing; she's havin' her own baby, soon."

"That's one of the tough things about this job," he observed. "We're the ones who find out the bad news first, and then we have to break it to the people who will suffer the most."

"One of the many tough things," she agreed, and—seeing an opportunity—added, "Which reminds me, Gabriel; if you ever need any help, or support—not just as one of those group-sponsor things, but in general—please don't be embarrassed to say. I truly want to help."

"I appreciate that," he said easily. "So far, so good."

He clearly didn't wish to speak of it, but there was nothin' for it; Doyle needed to hear his answer to the next question. "Are you managin' to stay clean?"

"I am," he replied, and it was the truth.

Doyle smiled. "I'm so glad to hear it. I hope you don't think I'm intrudin'—I should have offered my help long before now."

"Not to worry; I understand. You never know whether it's better to intrude, or not to intrude."

"Exactly." It was on the tip of her tongue to say that this was also what Munoz had said, but then Doyle remembered that she shouldn't mention Munoz, and so instead she offered, "But we're friends, Gabriel, and that's what makes it different. Friends should share each other's burdens, whether it intrudes or not."

He smiled at her, rather ironically. "If only it were so simple, Sergeant."

A bit surprised by the surge of mixed emotions she felt emanating from him, she insisted, "It's only complicated because we make it so. We can't put embarrassment, or hurt feelings above a friendship—friends are supposed to bear one another's burdens."

"I will concede the point. And I do appreciate it."

Clearly, he didn't want to discuss his troubles, and so Doyle admitted, "Sorry. My husband's your boss, and I'm clompin' about like a cow in a corn-field."

With a sudden display of genuine warmth, he smiled at her. "You may clomp about in my corn-field any time, Sergeant."

"I don't know how else to be," she admitted. "Which is why I'm that ashamed that I haven't been more helpful. Faith, I feel the same way about Martina Betancourt; she's bein' held at Wexton Prison until her preliminary, and I can't speak with her, or even send a message. She's my friend too—or at least, she was, until—until the donnybrook."

He tilted his head. "She's probably being held in psych; you've no chance of seeing her, even if you wanted to climb over the razor-wire fencing."

She sighed. "I know. But at the very least I should go church and pray for her—shame on me, for not doin' it sooner."

He leaned back in his chair, and teased, "Did you pray for me, too, when I was locked away?"

"I did," she assured him. "I still do."

"I appreciate it," he said, with a slight bow of his head. "I sincerely do; I hope you don't think I'm mocking you."

"I think there's a bit of mockin', thrown in," she admitted.

With a shrug, he confessed, "I'm too cynical for my own good, I suppose. I met your priest at St. Michael's Church, back when I was serious about Munoz. I wondered whether I could make a go of it."

This was of interest, and so Doyle ventured, "And what did you think?"

He spread his palms. "I'm not much of a believer in anything, I'm afraid. It would take a burning bush, or something equally dramatic."

She smiled slightly. "Father John once told me that mankind is always lookin' for signs and wonders, not realizin' that we're hip-deep in signs and wonders all the while."

"I suppose that's one way to look at it."

Doyle gazed out the window, and knit her brow. "Martina is somethin' of a religious zealot. I wonder what the psych ward will make of her."

He shrugged. "It doesn't matter; she can't get an unsound-mind defense, not with all the premeditation she'd done."

A bit absently, Doyle nodded in agreement. "D'you think they'll send her to Maghaberry?"

"I wouldn't think so," he replied, slightly amused by the question. "That one's for men—the worst of the worst."

"Oh—aye, you're right; I keep forgettin'. A nasty place, even though it's my home-country. Remember when Commander Tasza went missing-presumed-dead up there?"

"I won't soon forget."

Doyle grimaced. "If I were sentenced to serve time in such a place, it would bring on an unsound-mind in short order. Small wonder, that people try to escape, and then go missin' in the bogs."

"Well, Maghaberry's an easy place to go missing from, since if you're there in the first place, no one's going to miss you very much. Keep your nose clean, Sergeant, and thus be spared the experience."

"Commit no major crimes," she agreed. "Mental note."

CHAPTER 29

I'm all a'quiver, like a rabbit's whiskers, Doyle thought a bit crossly, as she made her way from Gabriel's office over to Acton's. I keep picking up crosscurrents from everyone I talk to today—first Munoz, and now Gabriel—and I've no idea why, or how to sort it all out. What is the point in quivering, for the love o' Mike, if you've no idea why? It's enough to drive one mad, which is why I should spend the bulk of my time lying low with little Edward, who has no undercurrents whatsoever, even though he is strangely obsessed with dinosaurs.

"Ho, Nazy," she greeted Acton's assistant as she approached from down the hall. "Your favorite pest is back yet again."

"You are not a pest, Officer Doyle," Nazy offered with a smile. "And the Chief Inspector should return soon; if you'd like, you may wait in his office."

Doyle pretended to consider this. "Best not. What if I rifle through his desk drawer, and find snaps of his girlfriend? Very awkward—he'd probably give us both the sack."

"You are teasing me, I think," the girl replied with a smile.

"I am indeed." Not quick on the uptake, was our Nazy, and Doyle always had the sneaking suspicion that this was exactly why Acton had hired her for the position.

The girl lowered her voice. "Sir Vikili again asked for a conference on the Betancourt case, but the Chief Inspector could not accommodate him today. I feel so badly, having to tell him this."

Doyle shrugged a shoulder. "Well, all honors to him for bein' persistent; when you're goin' to lose the case on the merits, then the next best thing is to beg for favors on bended knee. No favors to be had from Acton, though; he's not a favor-giver so much as he's an un-favor-giver, if there is such a thing. He holds a grudge like no other."

Oh, Doyle thought suddenly, lifting her head. Oh—that's important—

Nazy regarded her in surprise. "Does the Chief Inspector hold a grudge against Sir Vikili?"

Quickly, Doyle re-focused her thoughts and assured the girl, "I was just gabblin', Nazy; pay me no mind." Faith, the last needful thing was for Nazy to repeat such a thing to her idol; a defense team could raise quite the ruckus if there was the slightest hint of personal grudge-taking by law enforcement—

"Here is the Chief Inspector," Nazy announced, as Acton stepped out from the lift.

"I'm hauntin' the hallways, sir," Doyle informed him cheerfully. "All my assignments keep windin' themselves up before they barely get started."

"Would they all did," he replied.

"Would that everyone would just stop murderin' each other."

"That, too," he agreed. "No calls, please."

"Yes, sir," said Nazy.

With no further ado, Acton put a hand on Doyle's back and ushered her into his office.

Doyle could barely contain herself until he closed the door behind them. "I'm on pins and needles, husband; what did Howard have to say?"

Acton cut to the nub as he leaned against his desk, and crossed his arms. "He was thoroughly shocked, and it seemed genuine to me."

She nodded thoughtfully. Although she'd an advantage in such things, a seasoned Chief Inspector would have his own sense of who was being truthful and who was not, and Acton was as seasoned as they came.

Her husband continued, "He's desperate to play it down, and wants a DNA test on the infant. If the child isn't his, he may have a chance of keeping it quiet."

Doyle made a sound of skepticism. "Graspin' at straws, I think. Lady Abby must have been certain that the baby was his, if she's a schemin' trollop worthy of the name. So; I gather you don't think he killed her?"

Acton lifted his head, and gazed out the window thoughtfully. "If I had to choose, I'd say 'no.'"

"Well, that's a relief, all in all. Could he offer any leads?"

"No. He didn't know if she was seeing anyone, and it does seem unlikely, given her fixation on him."

Doyle considered this, her brow knit. "Any chance that it was staged—that she staged it, to get 'im in trouble?"

He turned his thoughtful gaze to her. "Explain, please."

Doyle frowned, trying to decide what it was she was

trying to say. "She was mad as a hatter, Michael, and wasn't makin' any progress in stealin' Howard away from Mary. Mayhap in a fit of thwarted love, she killed herself, and tried to frame him out of spite."

Acton tilted his head. "It seems unlikely, to me. Recall that her trump card was the baby; at the very least she could go public, and seek her revenge in that way without having to kill herself."

"Aye," Doyle conceded. "Sorry—I'm not sure why I suggested such a thing; she never struck me as bright enough to stage a misdirection murder, in the first place—let alone her own misdirection murder."

He reached to take her hands in his and pull her to him. "You have excellent insights, Kathleen, as I well know."

She sighed. "Not this time, I don't. So, what's next?"

"I've asked Lizzy Mathis to do a discreet, rapid-DNA test on the child, using Howard's profile. We'll have the local detective team see if her relatives can offer anything of interest, but I doubt it; by all accounts they were estranged, and may not have even been aware of the child's existence."

"Poor mite," said Doyle with all sincerity. "If Lady Abby's family doesn't want to take him in, he'll be shuttled into Child Protection Services."

Acton's gaze met hers. "You may be forgetting the other side of the equation."

She stared at him, as the penny dropped. "Oh—oh, that he's Howard's, of course. Which means our Mary will take him in at the drop of a hat, because that's who she is. Faith, she'll have two infants, and we'd lose her for certain. Which means I will probably have to take to drinkin' heavily."

He nodded. "It is unfortunate, but I imagine you are

correct. We'll stay in a holding pattern, however, until the DNA results are established."

Doyle ventured, "So Mary doesn't know about the baby?

"Not as yet."

"I'm not a very good keeper-of-secrets," she confessed rather anxiously.

He drew her into an embrace. "It won't be for long, I imagine. This is not the kind of secret that will keep."

"Poor Mary," she said, and rested her head against his chest. "That sword-fellow is holding his sword over her poor head, and she's all unknowin'."

"Damocles," he supplied.

Startled by the nuance in his tone, she drew back to look up at him. "What is it?"

He regarded her in surprise. "What is what?"

Lowering her head back to his chest, she said, "Nothin'. Those bloodthirsty Greeks give me the willies, is all."

But it was strange; she'd thought she'd sensed something in his voice, when he said the Greek-fellow's name, but it made no sense whatsoever that Acton would be emanating satisfaction about a sword hanging over poor Mary's head— her poor brain must be muddled.

"Oh," she said, reminded." There are two things I wanted to ask you, and I should have written them down, because I can only remember one."

"Then let's hear the one."

She lifted her head to gaze up at him again. "Is Munoz in the soup? I hear you met with her, a few days ago."

There was a small pause. "If she were," he replied slowly, "I am afraid I would not be at liberty to tell you."

She lowered her head again. "No, I suppose not." This

was disappointing, but on the other hand, it also seemed to confirm Nazy's impression that something was afoot.

"Has Munoz said anything to you?"

Surprised, she lifted her head yet again. "No, she hasn't, and you're bein' mighty mysterious, my friend." Suddenly alert, she asked suspiciously, "Never say she's gettin' promoted?"

"If she were—again—I would not be at liberty to tell you."

Thoroughly annoyed, Doyle groused, "Like you're one to give two pins about the protocols, husband."

"Speaking of which, Father John phoned to ask whether we would do the readings at Midnight Mass."

Doyle decided she'd allow him to distract her—if he didn't want to talk about Munoz, it wasn't going to happen—and so she replied, "And what did you say?"

"I told him we hadn't yet decided if we would be in town."

"Oh—oh, right." There it was again, Acton's desire to withdraw from here with all speed. She hadn't caught the sense that there was anything beneath Lady Abby's murder that would inspire this desire, though, so it may well be that he was just ready for a change of scenery. She certainly was—at least when one was living at Trestles, one could avoid venturing out into the miserable weather, and wander about the drafty halls, instead.

Reminded, she asked, "Can you truly bring-in some snow for Edward?"

"Indeed, I can," he replied, and bent to kiss her.

She smiled. "While you're at it, can you bring him a dinosaur? That would be top o' the trees, in his book."

CHAPTER 30

$\mathcal{D}$oyle came home to discover that Callie and Mary had taken Edward for a walk down the street, so as to admire the Christmas displays in the store windows.

"Ach—a shame I missed them; I should have texted that I was on my way, but I've got a case of pregnant-brain, and I'm havin' trouble rememberin' things. Mayhap I can catch-up to them."

"They should return soon, madam," Reynolds said, with an eye to the weather outside the windows. "It is coming rain, again."

With a sigh, Doyle settled into a kitchen chair, "All right; I'll wait here, although I wouldn't mind takin' a look at the decorations, myself, so as to get into the spirit o' things. I see you put a holly-bough on the door, Reynolds—thank you, I'd forgot. And we should bring-in a little tabletop Christmas tree—although I imagine Edward will still manage to pull it over, regardless of where we put it. We could hang it from the ceiling, mayhap? Or just accept fate, and hand him the family-crest ornaments, so that he can bowl them across the floor."

"Whatever you wish, madam," said Reynolds in a disapproving tone.

She smiled, and teased, "Just wait till there are two of them, Reynolds."

"I quite look forward, madam," he replied, and surprisingly, this was true. Or perhaps not so surprisingly; Reynolds was deeply invested in the aristocracy, and it was just as well he never got a glimpse of the ghosts at Trestles, who were a sorry excuse and always quarreling amongst themselves over the most ridiculous things—honestly; who cared who was looted by who, three hundred years ago? Talk about murder-in-material-gain, that lot took the palm, with no insult too trivial to be an excuse to go to war, and carry off as much as they could steal.

Oh, she thought, suddenly struck. "Reynolds, where is that sapphire necklace, now? It's back from the pawn shop, I hear."

Reynolds paused in extreme surprise. "A *pawn* shop, madam?"

"Oh—oh, sorry, I was just jokin'. Is it here, or has Acton thrown it into the vault at Trestles?

"I believe Lord Acton keeps it in the safe here, madam."

"Next to my tiara," she teased. "Poor thing, I should dust it off and parade around with it on Christmas Day, just to entertain Edward."

The butler ventured, "It is my understanding that you will be at Trestles on Christmas Day, madam."

Oh, thought Doyle, carefully keeping her gaze downcast. Is that a bit of longing, I hear? "Is there any chance," she asked casually, "that you could come along, Reynolds? I'm not one for wassailin', and such, and I'd need someone in my corner."

Carefully hiding his leap of pleasure, the butler demurred, "I imagine Mr. Hudson would not appreciate having me underfoot, madam."

Hudson was the Steward of Trestles, which was—as near as Doyle could figure—a position similar to that of the Pharaoh's cup-bearer. "Nonsense, Reynolds; you know he appreciates your help—especially with Acton's mother." It was true; Reynolds was a past master at soothing elderly harridans. With all sincerity, she added, "I wouldn't want to be selfish, though, and interrupt your own plans."

"I can re-arrange my plans, if need be," the servant said generously.

"Then that's grand; make sure to pack my tiara for the trip."

"Certainly, madam."

Doyle mused, "I don't know how they handle Christmas, but I would imagine the servants have the day off. I wonder if Callie will be able to lend a hand with Edward, since she's from that area?"

"I do not know Miss Callie's plans, madam."

But Doyle wasn't listening, because she'd suddenly realized that this was what she'd forgot—she'd forgot to tell Acton that she thought Callie was uneasy about Savoie, for some reason. Although to be fair, girls her age tended to be uneasy about trivial matters, and it could easily be that she was making a mountain out of a molehill. Her problems certainly couldn't hold a candle to poor Mary's, who was about to be hit with a brickbat of bad news.

Thus reminded of the secret-baby development, Doyle sighed as she waited for the nanny to answer her text. "We'll not have Mary much longer, I'm afraid, and it's a mournful shame, but life moves on, and we can't keep everythin' just the way we'd like. Fate steps in, like that sword-fellow from the Greek stories."

Reynolds paused. "Sword-fellow, madam?"

She lifted her face to address him. "You know the one, Reynolds; he's lurkin' about to clobber you over the head when you least expect it. Nemsemis, or somethin'."

But the servant could not allow this mischaracterization to pass, and explained, "If you are referring to the Sword of Damocles, madam, that allegory a bit different. In his case, the sword represents the constant fear of reprisal, for those who are in power."

She regarded him for a moment. "Not a clue, Reynolds. Translate into English, please."

The butler amended, "A king can never rest easy, because his enemies are always coming for him."

"Oh," she said with a knit brow. "Well that's interestin', and not at all what I thought it was. I'd thought it applied somehow to Acton and this case, but that doesn't make much sense, because I don't think her murder has anythin' to do with any power struggles between kings."

The servant was understandably at sea. "Whose murder, madam?"

Suddenly reminded that she was supposed to keep her lip buttoned, Doyle only said vaguely, "It's a case that Acton's workin', where we're not even sure that it's a murder. He's the one who brought up that Damocles-person."

"I'm afraid I need a bit more information, madam."

"Me, too," she agreed thoughtfully. "Me, too."

Mary texted to say they were returning to the flat due to

the rain, and asked if Savoie and Emile could come up for cocoa, since they'd all been walking together.

Doyle texted her acquiescence, and then said, "Batten the hatches, Reynolds; the crew is comin' up, and they'll be wantin' to be fed—Savoie and Emile, too." With a guilty start, she asked, "Do we happen to have a birthday cake, lyin' about? I forgot Emile's birthday, last week."

"I will enlist the concierge, madam, and have one delivered *sub rosa*."

Doyle regarded him in all admiration. "You'd make a good detective, Reynolds."

"Indeed, madam."

Pausing, Doyle was reminded that Reynolds had already proved his mettle in *sub rosa* work, and that perhaps she shouldn't be raising such a subject, what with Savoie coming up to the flat, bold as brass. I've far too many secrets to keep, she thought crossly; I don't know how Acton manages it.

CHAPTER 31

*D*oyle needn't have worried, however, because she'd forgot that Savoie behaved in an altogether different manner when he was with his son, Emile. It was the eighth wonder of the world, that the notorious Frenchman doted on his adopted child, and rather than exhibiting his usual careless, provocative manner, Savoie was instead focused on minding the boy, who tended to be a bit boisterous.

"Don't you celebrate Christmas?" Emile asked, as he cast an eye around the main room. "My papa says that some people don't celebrate Christmas."

"We do," Doyle assured him a bit guiltily. "I just haven't had time to decorate for it, as yet."

"We have a *huge* tree—Papa had to cut off the top, because it was too tall for the room." He turned to address Gemma, Mary's little girl, who was in the kitchen, helping Reynolds prepare the cocoa. "You should see it, Gemma."

"We have a Christmas tree, too," Gemma offered in her soft voice. "I made a paper star, at school."

"It's lovely," Mary declared.

"Is it awash in purple glitter?" asked Doyle.

Mary laughed. "Indeed, it is, Lady Acton. And Gemma's asked Father Christmas for new art materials, since we are running low."

"*Père Noël* is going to bring me a new bicycle," Emile announced, and then, with all good grace, accepted Edward's proffered dinosaur toy.

"Only if you behave," Savoie reminded his son.

Doyle teased, "You're wantin' a bicycle? I thought your Papa was going to buy you a horse, Emile; I think he's puntin' on his promises."

"A horse would not be practical," the boy replied, and it was clear that he was parroting his papa. "A bicycle makes much more sense, in the city." Idly, he made the dinosaur fly about, whilst Edward watched, equal parts delighted that the older boy was playing with his favorite toy, and worried that he wouldn't get it back.

"Doyle offered, "Well, there's horses at Trestles, and you can come ride them any time you like."

Emile brightened at this suggestion. "Can Miss Callie come?"

"She certainly can."

"Come, children," Reynolds announced. "Sit at the table, please."

"I'll take Edward, madam," said Callie, who deftly secured the dinosaur toy from Emile, and then passed it over to Edward, much to the smaller boy's general relief.

Savoie went into the kitchen to pour himself coffee, and so

Doyle said in an aside to Mary, "Emile's thrown you over for Callie, Mary; best look to your laurels."

The nanny laughed. "They love Miss Callie, and she's a wonderful girl, Lady Acton. Thank you so much for bringing her in."

Doyle ventured, "You may not want to come back to us after your maternity leave, Mary, and there's no one to blame you, so please don't feel as though you must. It's not as though you've got to earn your bread, anymore."

But the nanny only raised her brows in surprise. "Nonsense, Lady Acton; I'd miss it—I feel as though we're all family."

Because of course she did, and the fact that this particular "family" included assorted criminals rubbing elbows with aristocrats didn't faze her one whit. She's so generous, Doyle thought, and inwardly winced at how that generosity would soon be tested by the revelation of her husband's loose-end child. On the other hand, Mary already had weathered such a test when Gemma came into her life, and the young woman had taken-in the little girl without so much as the blink of an eyelash.

I don't know as I'd be so generous, Doyle thought in all honesty. And I'm the odd one out, here; Savoie did much the same thing—he took in the child of his enemy without a second thought, and then moved heaven and earth to create a good life for the boy.

Doyle's gaze rested on Savoie, who leaned against the counter, watching the children spill their cocoa and squabble over the Christmas biscuits. He's very content, she thought; and who would have ever thought such a thing? He's rather like me and Mary; living a life that was completely off the radar-screen, a few short years ago. Faith; the only one here who's not a fish-out-of-water is Reynolds—Reynolds and Edward, I suppose. The rest of us are wondering how all this came about.

With an inward shake, she corrected herself; no—I know exactly how this all came about, and shame on me for not giving thanks in all things. Instead, I've been hanging back, and moping about as though I'd lost faith in the Divine Plan. Shame, shame on me.

With a determined smile, she turned to say to Mary, "We're bringin' in a birthday cake for Emile—better late than never. I'm that sorry I forgot he'd a birthday, or I would have come to the park with you to celebrate."

"Oh, no—it was only a little affair, Lady Acton." The other woman paused for a moment, and then lowered her voice. "I had to keep it quiet, because Nigel is worried about our spending time with Mr. Savoie; apparently, he has a criminal past."

In spades, thought Doyle, who nonetheless offered, "It seems unlikely that anyone is goin' to find out you gave Savoie's son a birthday party, Mary."

With a knit brow, the nanny confessed, "Nigel's—well, he's very worried about how things look, nowadays." She took a long breath. "He seems—I know I shouldn't say, Lady Acton, but Nigel has not been himself, lately. He's been meeting with Lady Abby. We had a row, but he said he felt it would be best to try to reason with her. He was worried that if he tried to get a restraining order, it would be in all the papers."

Now, here's a crackin' minefield, Doyle thought; and if I was any sort of detective, I'd ask some questions about exactly when those meetings were, but I can't bring myself to do it, not with poor Mary—she'll soon hear about the baby, and let's weather one disaster at a time. Besides, Acton truly doesn't think Howard murdered the wretched woman, so best not say anything that might plant that seed in her mind.

Instead, Doyle offered, "It's not his fault, Mary; he just got himself tangled up with the wrong woman."

Mary nodded. "Yes. I suppose I was angry about all the secrecy—that he hadn't been honest with me."

Since Howard had good reason to avoid being honest—in his own mind, at least— Doyle could only soothe, "I think they try to spare us, the husbands, and don't realize they're just makin' things worse, in the long run." She then paused in surprise, because her scalp had started prickling. What? Was Acton trying to spare her, and only making things worse? Not a surprise, of course—only see how he'd been stinting on her assignments lately, which had only led to her unsanctioned pawn shop visit, and the hornet's nest she'd kicked over—

With a smile, Mary readily agreed, "Yes—that's it, exactly. It comes from a good place, I suppose, and please pay no mind to my complaints."

Quirking her mouth, Doyle offered, "Faith, Mary; we need to blow off a bit o' steam, every now and again, lest we strangle them outright."

At this juncture, Reynolds announced Emile's birthday cake, and they all moved around the table to sing to the boy as he beamed with pleasure, with Callie pulling Edward back so that he wouldn't try to blow out the candles himself.

The ritual completed, Reynolds began slicing-up the cake, and Savoie addressed him with all gratitude. *"Merci, monsieur."*

"It was my pleasure, Mr. Savoie; we cannot allow such a happy occasion to pass unremarked."

Savoie lifted his head to address Mary across the table.

MURDER IN UNSOUND MIND

"Soon we will celebrate Mademoiselle Gemma's adoption, yes?"

Mary smiled with sheer happiness. "Indeed, we will, Mr. Savoie, and I'm so relieved." She explained to Callie, "We weren't able to adopt her before now, due to—well, due to her circumstances."

"All sorted out, now," said Doyle brightly, and carefully didn't look at either Savoie or Reynolds.

Savoie continued to address Mary. "You will let me know, yes? I will hold the party for Mademoiselle, when it is official."

"Why, that's a very kind thought, Mr. Savoie. I suppose it would be rather like a birthday, wouldn't it?"

"My birthday's not till September," Gemma ventured, understandably confused.

Mary leaned down to embrace the girl from behind. "It will be a family celebration, love."

"I don't get to have two birthdays," Emile complained. "It's not fair."

"Emile," warned Savoie.

"You had two parties," Gemma pointed out.

"Two," Edward repeated, because he wanted to contribute to the conversation.

"It won't really be a birthday," Mary explained to the boy. "There won't be any presents."

"Oh," Emile said, as his brow cleared.

"I'll let you have a slice of cake," Gemma offered generously.

"Not coconut," Emile warned.

"Not coconut," Gemma readily agreed. "Chocolate, with purple icing."

"Sounds tasty—I hope I get a slice, too," Doyle declared.

CHAPTER 32

*D*uring the impromptu party, Doyle watched for any hint of trouble between Callie and Savoie, but it seemed to her that neither of them was paying the slightest bit of attention to the other. Of course, Savoie would behave himself, here at the flat, but nevertheless, she didn't catch any whisper that the girl was uneasy in his presence. Nevertheless, Doyle decided she should take the opportunity to open the subject; she'd do it casually, and sound her out.

And so, when all the blue icing had been washed from Edward's face, and he'd been set on the floor to color with Gemma, Doyle wandered over to stand beside Callie. "Thank you for venturin' out, today, despite the cold. The boyo needs to burn off his energy."

"We didn't get very far," Callie admitted.

"Well, you can start goin' back to the playground at the park, if we are ever again blessed with decent weather. The Lady Abby situation has been resolved."

The girl looked at her in relief. "That's good news, Lady Acton. Poor Miss Mary was so upset."

"Well, I'm glad we were told about it, because the last thing we want is for a member of our household to feel uncomfortable, for any reason."

She paused, but the girl only nodded without giving any indication of consciousness, and so Doyle decided she should be a bit more direct. "You know, Callie, if anyone bothers you, you must let me know—I don't want you to feel pestered."

With some surprise, her companion agreed, "Right, Lady Acton. I would be sure to say."

Not yet certain that she'd a good sense about whether there was anything to worry about, Doyle added, "You're a pretty lass, and a man might feel he can't resist makin' the attempt."

Callie turned to stare at her in astonishment, and— belatedly seeing the implication of her words—Doyle hastily corrected, "Oh—oh faith; I'm not referrin' to Acton, and let this be a lesson to me not to beat around the bush. Instead I was wonderin' if Savoie's been botherin' you. Tell me plainly —don't be afraid to say."

The young woman continued to stare at Doyle in surprise. "Oh—no, ma'am. Nothing like that. I was only a bit surprised when he—well, when he—"

"When he what?" Doyle prompted. "Did he threaten Lady Abby?" Doyle knew from experience that Savoie could offer- up menacing threats with the best of them.

"No, ma'am. It was just—" she hesitated, and then said, "When they turned Lady Abby away, Mr. Trenton and Mr. Savoie seemed angrier with each other than with Lady Abby. I was worried that they'd come to blows."

It was Doyle's turn to stare at the girl in surprise. "Savoie and *Trenton*? Truly?"

"Yes, ma'am."

Thinking over this unexpected revelation, Doyle came up with what seemed to be the obvious explanation. "Mayhap they each had their own idea about how to control the situation, and didn't like any interference from the other—they each thought they knew how to handle it." Alpha-lions, doing what they did best; indeed, this was why police work had a strict hierarchy of command—they couldn't allow every officer involved to decide they knew best how to address a dangerous situation.

"That must be it," the girl agreed, but Doyle could see that she was not convinced.

As they stood and watched the children, Doyle considered what the girl had told her. Savoie and Trenton apparently didn't like each other, which was interesting, since Trenton was a loyal Acton foot-soldier, and presumably, he was aware that Savoie was himself allied with Acton. The two men were not very much alike, though, and such things happened—faith, there were officers at work who couldn't stand each other, after all. Humans beings were human—not exactly a news flash.

Their conversation was interrupted when Acton came through the door, and paused on the threshold to review the chaotic scene.

"The Mongol hordes have invaded," Doyle informed him. "Enter at your own risk."

He smiled and came over to kiss her, no easy feat since Edward had attached himself to one of his legs like a limpet. "So, I see."

"Did you text?" she asked a bit guilty. "My mobile's somewhere around here."

"No matter," he said, as he hoisted-up Edward. "Is that cake?"

"Indeed, sir," said Reynolds, who hurriedly went to salvage a piece from the wreckage.

Gemma announced importantly, "It's Emile's birthday, again."

"I've had two," the boy announced. "Just like Gemma."

"I've had two," Edward parroted the older boy, and tried to hold up three fingers.

"Excellent, all around," Acton replied.

And here's another person who's living an unexpected life, Doyle thought with an inward smile. A few years ago, Acton would have taken great pains to avoid walking into a scene such as this—faith, I would have balked at it, myself—and yet here we are, knee deep in blue, sticky fingers.

As she went to join him at the table, she offered, "I'm that sorry I was off the grid, Michael." He checked in with her often, and tended to worry when she didn't respond—'worry' being a nicer way of saying that he didn't handle it well, at all, which was presumably why he'd hurried home. After all, the last time he hadn't been able to raise her on the phone she'd been fighting like a tigress on the stairway.

"No matter; I can see that you were busy." He handed-off Edward to Callie, and then settled in beside Doyle at the table, where his cake waited. "How are you feeling? Your color is much better today, Kathleen."

"Meanin' I'm red as a beet, from the candles, and such. But I do feel much better—my appetite's back." To emphasize this point, she took the opportunity to sneak a quick bite of his cake. "I'm that sorry I brought you home early, Michael; I didn't mean to make you worry."

"I needed to give you a warning, is all."

She paused in stealing another bite, because this ominous statement was belied by the fact that he didn't seem overly-concerned, as he took his own bite. "Oh-oh," she said. "What sort of warnin'?"

He glanced over at her. "I wanted to make certain you didn't say anything about the baby to Mary, since the rapid-DNA results show there is no match."

She lowered her fork to stare at him in abject surprise. "Oh—oh, Mother a' *Mercy*, but there's a twist in the plot. And what a relief; Howard's off the hook."

Acton tilted his head with mild disagreement as he allowed her to take another bite. "Not necessarily; he didn't know the baby wasn't his, when Lady Abby died."

"But he can better smother the story now—assuming that he didn't do her in, of course, since that would be a story that can't be smothered." She slid him a glance.

Naturally, Acton was not going to commit to such a law-abiding statement, and so instead he demurred, "We have yet no indication that he's a suspect. I'm of two minds about whether I should go speak to Sir Stephen."

Doyle stared at him yet again. "Holy Mother, Michael; d'you think *Sir Stephen* killed the wretched woman?"

"I think it very unlikely," he replied, and it was true. "But I should break the news to him, and find out if he has any insights. Unfortunately, it would mean he'd know that the police were involved in Lady Abby's death, and that such information would embarrass Howard, if it became public."

"Aye," she said, seeing his point. "It's hard to know if it's worth questionin' him, for the trouble he could cause."

"Indeed."

"Are you goin' to have that last bite?"

"It is yours."

As she scraped the final trace of blue icing from the plate, she glanced up at him sidelong. "So; I'm to say nothin' to Mary about any of this? What if the coroner decides to hold an inquest?"

"I think we should wait, for the time being. And any revelations should best be made by Howard, in any event." He looked over to Reynolds, and called out. "Another piece of cake, if you would."

"Certainly, sir."

"There won't be any left-over to pack up," Emile ventured in a worried tone.

"Emile," warned Savoie.

"I will have another cake sent over to your house, Master Emile," Reynolds offered smoothly. "If that is all right with your father."

"Why does Emile get *three* cakes?" asked Gemma, who clearly thought this unfair.

"We'll need a cake, too, Mr. Reynolds," Mary told the butler with a smile. "Chocolate with purple icing, please."

CHAPTER 33

*T*hat night, Doyle found herself facing Dr. Harding, and yet again, he seemed reluctant to start the conversation, and so she decided to address a niggling worry that she couldn't seem to shake. "I've the feelin'—I've the feelin' that Acton is the one holdin' the danglin' sword, but that doesn't make much sense, given what we know about the facts on the ground. There aren't any kings, fightin' against each other."

"Very good," Dr. Harding said in an approving tone.

Doyle stifled an annoyed response, and instead gathered up the shreds of her patience. "What's 'very good'?"

"You are reasserting your cognitive functions."

She frowned a bit, guessing at what this meant, and admitted, "Aye. I was off-kilter, for a bit. Foggier than even my usual—I had a lot of trouble rememberin' things."

He didn't respond, and so she joked, "Pregnant-brain."

Since there was still no response, Doyle offered, "And speakin' of off-kilter, I'm finally goin' over to the church tomorrow to pray for poor Martina—better late than never. She's gone off-kilter much worse than me, and now she's a bleak future ahead of her."

"Savior complex," he pronounced. "A classic case."

Her brow knit, Doyle thought this over. "Well, yes—I suppose, what with the whole righteous-crusader thing she does. Although she wasn't much of a righteous-crusader for Antonio's girlfriend, which only goes to show how far off the deep end she's gone."

"The woman's death is an anomaly," he agreed.

Because she wasn't certain what the word meant, Doyle ventured, "You know, you're always sortin' people into psychiatrist-slots, Dr. Harding, but I don't think people are so easily sorted out. Martina—Martina's not your run-of-the-mill unsound-mind. Faith, I wish I could speak with her, and find out why she did it."

"You are unable," he noted. "You are stymied."

Doyle took a guess at what 'stymied' meant, and replied, "Yes—I suppose I am. It's ironic, all in all; she may not have an unsound-mind legal defense, but they've locked her down tight, regardless, and it must be quite a blow, to someone like her, who's used to doin' whatever she wishes to do, and goin' wherever she wishes to go. I should go offer comfort to the imprisoned, like you're supposed to—it's one of the 'good works' they ask you to do. And especially at Christmas—it's a time to do good works, to show that you understand the point of it all."

"But you cannot see her," the psychiatrist reminded her. "You are stymied."

Doyle nodded. "Right; so instead I'll go offer up my prayers, and while I'm at it, I'll ask forgiveness for bein' so absorbed in nursin' my own hurts that I've been neglectin' the 'good works' requirement."

Her companion tilted his head to the side in mild disagreement. "You've experienced a trauma, and certainly can be forgiven your distraction."

But Doyle shook her head. "No—'tis the season of charity and good works, and I'm runnin' well-behind, in that department. Not to mention that it's my job to make Christmas magical for Edward—the same as my mother made it magical for me. Shame on me, for mopin' about, and lickin' my wounds—my mother had her own massive problems, yet she managed it."

She paused, suddenly struck. "I think that's what bothers me most about that stupid Magi-story—the one about the husband and wife. There's no charm in scrapin' to sacrifice, when there's no money to be had. Livin' hand-to-mouth is not charmin' at all, no matter what the writers may think, as they write their stories in their snug little houses. Lookin' back, I think my mother only pretended she liked the snow— it only made our lives harder, and our lives were hard enough."

"Not true," her companion disagreed. "She loved the snow, and she never allowed the cold in."

Doyle thought this over for a moment, much struck by his choice of words. "No, she never allowed the cold in—because of me, I suppose. At the time, I never saw how hard it was for her."

"Do you think she would rather not have had you, and lived an easier life?"

"Never," said Doyle immediately, surprised by the question. "We were everythin', to each other. It truly wasn't a sacrifice, a'tall."

"Very good," he said.

With a mighty effort, Doyle stifled a sharp retort, and steered him back to the topic at hand. "But what's Acton up to? I feel as though there are more than a few swords about to fall, and that I should be payin' better attention than I am."

"Yes," he agreed. "The sword is the key, of course."

Impatiently, Doyle explained, "I wasn't speakin' about the *real* sword; I was speakin' of that Greek-fellow."

"One and the same," said the psychiatrist. "One and the same."

And then Doyle found that she was suddenly awake, staring at the darkened bedroom wall, and listening to her husband's even breathing.

CHAPTER 34

On her way into work the next morning, Doyle stopped by St. Michael's to say her neglected prayers for the various people who had need of them. The altar was decorated for Christmas, and Doyle sat in the front pew and breathed in the scent of pine, feeling an almost unbearable tightness in her breast, as she was reminded of Christmases past, in a simpler time.

Her thoughts were interrupted when Father John slid in beside her, and observed with a great deal of pride, "Are you admirin' our new nativity scene, Kathleen?"

Acton had donated a beautiful Italian-porcelain nativity scene, because the old wooden one was the worse for wear, not to mention that the figure of the Blessed Mother had been dropped on some long-ago occasion, and so was missing part of her arm.

"It's lovely, indeed," she replied. "I'm sorry I missed the decoratin' committee, Father—I've been that busy."

"No matter, child. Are you here to say a rosary for your mother?"

"I will, Father, but just now I'm prayin' for Martina Betancourt, who's lost her bearings, even though she's the last person you'd ever think would lose her bearings. Faith, if she were a man, she'd be a priest, or a Crusader, or somethin'. Unfortunately, she fell in love with a wrong-un, and it's addled her brain."

Father John sighed. "Now, there's a shame."

Slowly, Doyle nodded, thinking this over. "The psychiatrists like to put people into little slots, sayin' they're a 'classic' this, or a 'classic' that, but I think it's miles more complicated than that. People are complicated beings, and Martina's a perfect example. I'd never think—never in a million years—that she'd take to murderin' trollops to soothe her own pride; she knows better than that. If nothin' else, I should go give her a good scoldin'."

"We are called to admonish the sinner," the priest agreed. "It is one of the Seven Spiritual Works of Mercy."

Doyle knit her brow as she turned to regard him. "But aren't we also called to comfort the imprisoned?"

"That's one of the Seven Corporal Works of Mercy," he explained. "Two different lists."

Doyle turned her palms up in her lap. "Then how do you reconcile the two, I ask you? I'm supposed to be comfortin' and admonishin' her at the same time?"

But the priest remained unfazed. "Aye—only see how the Prison Ministry does it. The sinner is comforted by the knowledge that there is hope of redemption, and forgiveness of sins."

Doyle lifted a corner of her mouth. "Well, that would be a tall order, Father, and I wouldn't know where to start, with

Martina. She'd be defiant, because she thinks she has 'just cause' to go about killin' people—although she'd have no 'just cause' argument for this last murder; it was a spite-murder, plain and simple."

But the priest only persisted, "Nevertheless, the blessin' of forgiveness would still stand, child, and the sinner should be made aware of this. It is what we are called to do—especially during this holy season."

With some reluctance, Doyle nodded. "Aye. Well, there's no way I can speak with her—she's locked down in custody, and so the next best thing is to pray that she'll right herself. I should have done it before now, but she's the reason we had the donnybrook at the flat, so I suppose I wasn't feelin' very charitable towards her."

Father John laid a hand on hers, where it rested in her lap. "Forgiveness is the hardest of all the Works of Mercy, lass—to forgive those who've grievously wronged us. We're only human, after all."

"Exactly," she agreed. "My mother used to say, 'much easier to tear than to mend'. It's not an easy thing, to forgive and forget."

"No one expects us to forget," the priest corrected. "Only to forgive."

Much struck, Doyle thought this over. "It would be miles easier to forgive if we could forget, though—just wipe it from our minds. I think that's the problem; we can't help but hold on to the bitterness, and replay our hurts over and over again."

Father John nodded. "Exactly this, lass; that's always the crux of it. We dwell on all the wrongs done to us, when we are supposed to let them go. Let St. Thomas More serve as an example; he told the jury who'd condemned him to death that he hoped they'd all meet-up again in heaven, and make merry together."

Doyle smiled slightly. "Well, he's a saint, Father. I don't know as I'm there, yet."

"Aye, lass. Which is why forgiveness is the hardest Work of all; we are called to bear wrongs patiently."

Her hand had started tingling, and so surreptitiously, Doyle tucked it beneath her other arm. "Easier said than done, Father; they were goin' to take Edward—take him straight out of his nursery, so that I'd never see him again. What sort of people would do such a thing? It's hard to imagine such evil, let alone forgive it."

The priest sighed. "We live in a fallen world, Kathleen, and it's beyond our ken to understand why such things are allowed to happen. The most we can do is stay in faith, and remember that there's a light in the darkness—especially at this time o' year."

Doyle took a steadying breath. "Well, the light seems mighty faint, sometimes, and the darkness mighty dark. It's easy to talk about your faith, and all your righteous principles, but it's a lot harder to live them out, in real life."

"No one knows this better than a priest, lass."

She smiled slightly at his tone, and they sat together in companionable silence for a few minutes, until she added, "D'you remember Officer Gabriel? I think he's right; it would be miles easier if we were treated to the occasional signs and wonders, just to help us along."

"You're awash in 'em, lass," the priest reminded her gently, his gaze resting on the porcelain figures set out before them. "You're awash in 'em."

CHAPTER 35

$\mathcal{F}$eeling immeasurably better, Doyle went in to work and—with renewed determination—made her way up to Gabriel's office to confer. Not only was Lady Abby's death still under investigation, she now had a second reason to check-in with him, in the form of a ghost who seemed to think the pawn-shop sword was the key to something. Best find out what—the ghosts never brought up things without a reason, even Dr. Harding, who seemed to wander-off onto topics that had little to do with her current caseload, such as how her mother dealt with her problems.

"Ho, sir," Doyle said, as she greeted Gabriel from his office door. "Tell me you've found someone else to do the slog work for the Lady Abby case."

"I will," he said, looking up. "The slogger is none other than your esteemed husband."

"*Acton* is reviewin' CCTV tape?" she asked in some surprise.

He motioned her in. "He is indeed. I took a preliminary

look 'round, but there wasn't much to see, due to the weather. There were two 'possibles' of a man walking with a blonde-looking woman, but nothing was clear, since everyone's geared up against the weather. Here, have a look for yourself."

Doyle squinted as she reviewed the dim figures, bundled up and obscured by umbrellas, as they walked along the embankment. "Fah, there's little enough there. Any vehicles that can be attached to either group?"

"I showed what I had to DCI Acton, who tells me he will see about image enhancements, and look for possible attached-vehicles."

This, said in a wooden tone that carefully didn't express what they were both thinking—that if Howard's car was attached to either couple, it would turn into a rare tangle-patch, which was no doubt why the esteemed DCI was swooping in to take over the slog work.

Frowning with this thought, Doyle shook her head slightly. "Faith, Gabriel; if Howard's at all involved, I'd be very much surprised. But then again, I've been surprised before."

He leaned back in his chair to regard her thoughtfully. "Speaking of such, there's a rumor going around that Sir Vikili is himself attached to something unsavory."

She'd the sense that his interest was very sharp, beneath his casual attitude, and she looked over at him in surprise. "D'you mean he's involved in somethin' *personally*?"

He shrugged. "Have you heard anything?"

Slowly, Doyle shook her head. "No. His brother was a piece of work—God have mercy on his wretched soul—and Sir Vikili's clients are *always* attached to somethin' unsavory, but I've not heard a whisper that the great man himself is sailin' too close to the wind." Curious, she asked, "Why, what have you heard?"

Gabriel demurred, "I shouldn't say—it may be nothing," and interestingly enough, this wasn't true.

Her curiosity piqued, Doyle offered, "I will see what I can find out, although Acton doesn't always tell me things, with Munoz's situation servin' as a prime example."

Her companion's dark brows rose. "Which Munoz-situation is that?"

"Oh-oh," she exclaimed, aghast. "My wretched, gabblin' tongue. Forget I said anythin'; it's like what you said about Sir Vikili, it may be nothin', and I shouldn't be tellin' tales."

"Not to worry," he said easily. "Already forgot."

This, of course, wasn't true and Doyle could only hope that Munoz's former beau would use some forbearance—although it seemed to her that all the thwarted-love people lately were not so much inclined to forbearance as they were inclined to run amok.

Quickly changing the subject, she asked, "What's my assignment, then?"

"I'm afraid to give you another assignment, Sergeant, because you keep stepping on landmines, and thus interrupting my attempt to live a more peaceful life."

She laughed, and replied, "Well, we'll let Acton handle the 'rule-out' for Howard on the Lady Abby case—since that would be a landmine-in-the-makin'—but there must be *somethin'* I could do that won't turn your hair grey." Affecting a casual air, she asked, "Mayhap I should see if I can find anythin' on the charge-nurse case. I could go back to the pawn shop, to ask about who pawned that sword, in the first place. It wouldn't be much of a thread, but at least it's somethin'."

Gabriel shrugged. "I already questioned the fellow there, but it was a dead-end. Their CCTV tape had been overwritten already, and the ID given was fake."

The words were true, but there was something to his tone —something that make her antennae quiver, yet again. She ventured, "That seems a bit strange, that someone would use a fake ID to pawn a fancy sword."

But he only cocked an amused eyebrow at her. "Your naivete is refreshing, Sergeant."

"Oh—oh, unless it was stolen in the first place, of course." She paused, frowning. "I suppose I'm a knocker, for not startin' out from that assumption."

"A pawn shop in Fremont? Why ever would you make such an assumption?"

She smiled. "All right; no need to rub it in. Instead, mayhap I should check to see if any recent burglaries had a sword in the inventory—although that does seem a slim thread. I suppose we should probably just assume it wound up in the transient's hands because it was stolen, yet again."

Gabriel nodded his agreement. "I did ask the burglary unit to do a search of their inventories, but they couldn't find anyone claiming that such a sword had been stolen."

Again, she'd the uneasy sense that he wasn't telling her everything he knew, which seemed a bit odd—why would he withhold a possible lead? That, and Dr. Harding seemed to think the stupid sword was the key, for some reason. But before she could decide whether she'd sound completely daft if she kept at him about the sword, he said, "I asked forensics to give me a detailed summary of Lady Abby's electronics, but I would not be at all surprised if our slogger has exerted control there, too."

Doyle could only agree with this assessment. "I shouldn't

be surprised. D'you want me to see if I can winkle any information out of Acton?"

"It might work. You are much prettier than I am."

With a smile, she said, "All right; I'll give it a try, but I imagine if there was anythin' of interest we'd have already heard."

"No doubt," he agreed, and interestingly enough, this wasn't true.

CHAPTER 36

*D*oyle headed over to Acton's office, and fortunately she wasn't given the opportunity to yet again distract Nazy from her work, because when Acton spotted her, he motioned her in, whilst he was finishing-up a phone call.

Doyle plunked down in a chair and idly reviewed her husband as he made it clear to whoever was on the other end that the call was coming to an end—it sounded as though he was speaking to a subordinate, although Acton would use the same tone if he were speaking to the Prime Minister, so it was impossible to truly tell.

"Thank you; I will be here for the next half-hour."

As he rang off, she was suddenly aware that he'd been drinking again, although it was not something anyone else would notice—Acton was very, very private, and it was a wonder he even allowed the wife of his bosom to get the occasional glimpse of his workings.

Thinking on possible reasons for this mid-morning tipple,

she began without preamble, "Is it Howard, that you saw on the CCTV tape? Is that why you've commandeered the slog work, like a humble first-year?"

"No," he replied immediately. "I do not believe it is Howard."

This was the truth, and it gave her pause. "Well, I think Gabriel thinks you're coverin' for Howard."

"He may think what he wishes, but I am not," he repeated, and it was the truth. "I can find no evidence that would link Howard to Lady Abby's death."

In a practical manner, she pointed out, "Then you should quit takin' the evidence away from Gabriel, please. You can tell that he doesn't know what to make of it."

Acton fixed his gaze on hers. "There is," he admitted slowly, "another troubling aspect that I would like to rule-out, before I allow Officer Gabriel full rein."

Doyle leapt to the obvious conclusion, and breathed, "Mother a' *Mercy*—did *Sir Stephen* truly murder the wretched woman?"

"No," he assured her. "Hudson informs me that Sir Stephen was visiting Trestles, on the evening of her death."

This was of interest, and Doyle ventured, "I thought Sir Stephen was banned from darkenin' the door, at Trestles."

Acton clarified, "He was visiting my mother, at the Dower House."

She made a face. "Never a good report, that one is." Acton's mother had been involved in more than a few schemes with Sir Stephen as her willing accomplice—or vice-versa—and so it was never a good sign when those two had their heads together. It was just as well that Acton kept close tabs on his wretched cousin, because the man couldn't be trusted an inch.

With a small frown, she asked, "So what's the troublin' aspect, then, if it's not Sir Stephen?"

"Trenton may be involved."

Doyle blinked. "*Trenton?*"

He nodded, watching her reaction. "Yes. I believe Trenton harbors warm feeling for Mary."

Doyle assessed this bit of information for a moment, and then acknowledged, "That's not a surprise, I suppose— everyone does."

Acton admitted, "He's never said anything, it is only an impression I have."

Doyle immediately saw where the conversation was headed—after all, Acton would have kept this secret, too, save for the fact that he must need her help. "And the reason you're tellin' me this is because you'd like me to do a bit o' listenin', when you ask him a few questions."

He nodded. "If you wouldn't mind. I'd like to rule him out."

Suddenly reminded, she told him in a worried tone, "Oh —oh, listen to this, Michael; I remembered the other thing I couldn't remember to tell you, which was that Callie said Trenton started goin' at Savoie, when they were dealin' with Lady Abby in the park—goin' at him hard enough that she was worried they'd come to blows. It seemed so out-of-character, and I just put it down to a struggle to be in control. But if you think Trenton's sweet on Mary, mayhap Trenton was white-knightin', and didn't want Savoie there as a fellow knight."

Acton was silent for a moment, considering this information, and so Doyle respected the process for a few moments before venturing, "If Trenton's a suspect, then would the workin'-theory be that Trenton killed Lady Abby because she was harassin' Mary? That seems a bit far-fetched."

"It does," he agreed. "But I should rule-out that possibility, before Gabriel goes forward with the investigation."

This, of course, because it was very unlikely that Acton would turn-in one of his loyal vassals to the tender mercies of the Crown Prosecutors; instead, he'd work his usual magic so that Trenton never appeared on law enforcement's radar screen. Trenton would nevertheless be summarily transferred back to Trestles, no doubt; after all, the last needful thing was to have the House of Acton's security person be the type who'd go off half-cocked in such a fashion.

But she frowned at this thought, because it did seem too fantastic to be true. I'd be very much surprised, if our Trenton would attempt a spot of murder, all on his own, she decided; and the only thing that makes me the least bit uneasy is the fact that Acton seems to consider it a possibility. Of course, Acton's been working cheek-to-jowl with Trenton over the course of his career, and so mayhap he knows the man better than I do.

Her thoughts were interrupted when Acton came to a decision. "Let's go home for lunch, and I'll ask to confer with Trenton about security matters under the guise of revealing Lady Abby's death. We will include Adrian, also, so that it doesn't appear to be an interrogation." He looked at his watch. "We can't go quite yet; Williams wished to meet in-person, to confer with me about this case."

Doyle blinked in alarm, since the case wasn't Williams', it was Gabriel's, and therefore it wasn't clear why he would wish to confer—especially in person. In fact, such a request implied there was something he knew that he didn't want to tell Acton on-the-record.

"Mother a' Mercy, Michael," she breathed. "D'you think Williams knows somethin' about Trenton? Or Howard?"

"We shall see. Absent a confession, though, it would make little difference; I would be surprised if the prosecutors thought there was sufficient evidence to support a homicide investigation."

"With your connivance?" she asked a bit sharply.

Surprised by her tone, he met her gaze. "Not at all, Kathleen. You heard what the coroner said—even she couldn't be certain it wasn't 'misadventure'. Without more, we wouldn't have enough to support a warrant."

Contrite, Doyle bent her head to rub her fingers on her temples. "Sorry—I didn't mean to snap at you, Michael. Stupid Lady Abby; causin' just as much trouble in death as she did in life."

He came around to stand beside her, and run a soothing hand over her head. "Perhaps you should rest a bit this afternoon, after our lunch-meeting. You've nothing pressing on your docket."

"Unless the Trenton landmine explodes," she cautioned. "Nothin' like discoverin' that one of your vassals needs to be thrown into the dungeon."

He continued to stroke her head, which was not exactly as soothing as it should have been, since it was something he tended to do when he was worried. "You mustn't distress yourself, Kathleen. In fact, it may be a good idea for you to leave for Trestles a few days early—you could take Edwards and Reynolds, and I could meet you there as soon as I may."

With a small smile, she lifted her face. "Trestles has its

own vassal-trouble, Michael; what if your mother and Sir Stephen are plottin' to storm the castle?"

"I imagine Hudson is fully prepared to repel all invaders."

"A bit o' boilin' oil wouldn't go amiss," she agreed, but before there could be any further discussion, Nazy buzzed to say, "DI Williams to see you, sir, along with Ms. Mathis."

"Send them in, please."

As Williams and Lizzy filed into the office, Doyle stifled a flare of alarm—now what? They both had an aura of seriousness, and stoic determination. Mayhap Lizzy knew something about Trenton she was hesitant to reveal—Trenton was her cousin, after all, and if he was the murdering sort, this would create quite the dilemma for the young woman.

Apparently having made his own assessment, Acton met Doyle's gaze with an unspoken message, and Doyle immediately rose to leave. "I'll be goin' then, Michael; nice to see you, Lizzy."

"You can stay, Kath," Williams said quietly. "It's nothing you can't hear, too."

Oh-oh, thought Doyle; I'm half-inclined to bolt for the door anyway—I'm pig-sick of having to deal with crisises—crises?—whatever the wretched word was, and a lass could use some peace, for a change.

Williams turned his gaze to Lizzy, who nodded her encouragement, and tucked a hand into his elbow. "Lizzy was asked to do the rapid-DNA test on Lady Abby's child—"

Holy Mother, thought Doyle, with a sudden burst of clarity; *Holy, Holy Mother*. And just when you think you've a handle on everything, along comes a completely different sort of landmine.

"—and she was aware that I'd had a brief fling with the victim, around the time frame in question."

When he was escorting Lady Abby home from Dublin, Doyle realized, in all wonder. It's that "man-switch," again—faith, it's amazing that any of them can accomplish anything remotely productive.

"So, Lizzy asked me if she could make a comparison, and it turned out the baby is mine. I'd no idea of his existence, of course."

There was a small, still silence, and no one spoke.

Glancing at Lizzy, Williams covered her hand with his. "My wife and I would like to adopt him."

His "wife," Doyle thought, blinking back tears. Now, there's a small word with a lot of weight behind it. And until you've got one, you've no idea how much weight it carries; it's rather like the word "son."

"You may have to give me a few lessons, Lady Acton," Lizzy joked in her awkward manner.

"You'll be a natural, Lizzy," Doyle said softly. "Congratulations to you both."

CHAPTER 37

"*M*en are truly stupid," Doyle remarked as she drove home with Acton for their lunch-meeting. "It's a wonder, is what it is."

"Am I included in this assessment?" he asked in a mild tone.

"Yes, you are," she firmly replied. "If I suggested we stop over at a hotel for sex, you'd think it a brilliant idea, even though we've a basketful of pressin' problems."

"It *is* a brilliant idea," he admitted.

"Well, you'll have to possess your soul in patience, husband, because we have to know whether the man who's supposed to be guardin' our hen house has decided to kill the occasional chicken."

"Right, then."

She smiled at his tone, and mentally crossed her fingers that whatever had touched off this latest drinking binge would dissipate in the face of the aforesaid pressing problems. A black mood was hovering—she could sense it, despite his light words.

She glanced over at him. "Did you have any clue, about Williams bein' the father?"

"None."

"Well, it's lucky you sidestepped that particular tangle-patch—she made a run at you, too, if I can keep my schemin' trollops straight."

"It is fortunate indeed that I did not succumb."

Doyle made a wry mouth, as she gazed out the windscreen. "More like it was lucky for her—lucky she didn't wind up dead, like so many before her."

"Unfair," he protested mildly. "I am unjustly maligned."

She nodded. "Aye; it's one of those 'cause and correlation' exercises, like they teach you at the Crime Academy. Since any trollop worthy of the name is going to make a run at you, you can't be blamed every time they turn up dead—it would never hold up in evidence."

He was silent, and she made a mighty effort to rein-in her gabbling tongue, because she could sense that she wasn't helping matters. Something's up, she thought with a sense of disquiet; mayhap we *should* stop and have sex somewhere, so's that I can talk him down from the ledge.

"How does your hand?" he asked into the silence.

"My hand does fine." She pronounced it "foine," just to tease him. "And you're wanderin' off into nob-speak." This, to let him know she knew he'd been drinking, since he tended to be much more House-of-Lords when he was in his cups, which only showed you how much he restrained himself when he was around his working-class wife.

He reached to clasp her arm, gently. "I am so glad," he said. "I did worry."

Consumed with contrition, she covered his hand with her own, and offered, "I'm sorry I gave you such a scare, Michael. I've learned my lesson."

He made some comforting reply, but she wasn't listening, because her scalp had started prickling like a live thing. What? she thought, resisting the urge to rub her temples yet again. I did learn my lesson—faith, and what a miserable lesson it was, trying to hide my hurts from my overly-watchful husband. Lucky, I am, that there was no real harm done—aside from the drinking, of course. And the black mood that keeps hovering, around the fringes. Which seemed a bit strange, all in all, because she was fast on the mend, and you'd think he'd be that relieved—

"In the future," he ventured, "if you would keep me informed, I promise I will not make you feel uncomfortable for it."

She grimaced. "Faith, Michael; don't make me feel worse than I already do."

"I'll say no more, then," he replied.

She lifted his hand to kiss its back—sunk in remorse, he was, and she hadn't the heart to explain to him that the last needful thing was to keep him informed; he already thought the ghosts were a figment of her over-active imagination, and so if she truly kept him informed, not only would she never be able to outfox him, he'd probably have her locked down tighter than Martina was, with the only difference being that he'd lock himself away right beside her.

Reynolds had been forewarned about the working-lunch, and so he was all efficiency when they came into the flat, having set-up the table and banished Callie and Edward to the lower floor. "Let me take your coats, please; Mr. Trenton and Mr. Adrian are waiting in the drawing-room."

As Reynolds hung-up their coats in the hall closet, Doyle whispered to Acton, "I don't know as we have a 'drawin'-room.'"

"Let's indulge him," Acton whispered back. "I imagine he's been on the phone with Hudson." He paused. "I informed them that you and Edward will travel to Trestles ahead of me, and so preparations should be made."

Doyle nodded without speaking, because again, she'd the uneasy feeling that she was being ushered offstage; her husband seemed a bit too eager to pack her off to start the holiday. Not to mention that he didn't do well, if he was separated from her for any length of time—faith, even with his busy docket, he still managed to see her, several times a day. It all seemed a little ominous—that he wanted her well-away from here—and she wondered if there was in fact something unsavory about Trenton that he didn't want her to winkle-out. If it was more important than having the wife of his bosom within close proximity to that bosom, it must be serious, indeed.

Her disquieting thoughts were interrupted when the other men rose to greet them, Trenton as stoic as ever, with Adrian trying not to look self-conscious at being called up to have lunch with his employer.

"Good to see you both," said Doyle, to put them at ease and make it clear they weren't in the soup. "We thought we'd best touch base, because something rather unexpected has come up."

Acton put a hand under her elbow, which she realized was a caution not to say too much in front of Reynolds—not to mention that he probably wanted to handle this interrogation himself; faith, she needed to work on her situational-awareness, as they said in the Crime Academy, and try to hold her tongue—never an easy proposition for her, but even harder, lately.

After they were seated and served, the butler withdrew, and Acton began, "We have distressing news, I'm afraid. Lady Abby has died, and it appears she died the evening after the altercation at the park."

"She *killed* herself?" Adrian asked, unable to contain his reaction. "Wow."

"Does that surprise you?" Acton asked.

"How does Adrian know Lady Abby?" Doyle asked in confusion.

There was a small silence, and then Acton informed her, "Adrian was stationed in front of the building when Lady Abby came by to ask where Miss Mary had gone—she claimed she was a friend, looking for her."

"Adrian's been reprimanded, ma'am," Trenton assured her.

With a show of support, Doyle smiled at the younger man. "How were you to know? Lesson learned, Adrian."

"Yes, ma'am," he offered in a subdued tone.

That pesky man-switch, at it again, Doyle thought. Heaven help us all.

"Are you surprised to hear she'd taken her own life?" Acton repeated, and Doyle realized she'd made a first-year error, interrupting the flow of his interrogation. In the back-and-forth of conversation, oftentimes a suspect let down his guard, and she'd interrupted the flow—gabbling, yet again.

Adrian knit his brow for a moment, as he considered the question. "I don't know—she seemed so cheerful. She laughed a lot."

"Not when I saw her," Trenton offered with a touch of irony. "A regular screecher."

Thoughtfully, Acton turned his attention to Trenton. "Is that so? What did she say?" This, said in a mildly curious tone that belied the fact that Acton was honing in like a laser beam.

"She started shouting at Miss Mary straightaway—very angry, sir. She used foul language—called her a lot of names." He glanced at Doyle, with the implication that he'd rather not specify exactly what was said in front of her, which was rather sweet, considering Doyle had worked at a fishmonger's in Dublin, once upon a time.

Trenton concluded, "Mr. Savoie told her there was no call for that, and asked her to leave."

Acton shook his head slightly, in feigned amazement. "Extraordinary. Did she have a weapon?"

"Not that I saw."

"Did Savoie have to lay hands on her?"

"No, sir." He paused. "We closed ranks, and walked her back. Then she gave up and left."

Doesn't want to talk about his kerfuffle with Savoie, thought Doyle. No doubt he realizes, with hindsight, that it was not such a good idea to start pushing-chests with the likes of him; Savoie's won plenty a knife-fight.

"Was that the last you saw of her?"

This causal question was, of course, the crucial one, and Doyle lowered her gaze to the table.

"Yes, sir."

Doyle kept her hands folded in her lap as a signal to her husband that this was the truth—which was quite the relief, all in all.

But Acton was one to tie-up every little thread, and so he turned to say to Adrian, "How about you, Adrian? Did you have any contact with her, after the park?"

"No, sir," said Adrian. "Like Lady Acton said, I learned my lesson."

As Doyle's hands continued to stay still, Acton shook his head slightly. "An unfortunate young woman," he declared, and then turned the topic to the coming holiday schedule.

CHAPTER 38

*A*cton had returned to the office, and Doyle was preparing to leave for Trestles—she'd been tempted to let Edward nap in the car, but then decided that she needed some time to get organized, anyway, and so they would leave after he woke up, even though it meant the drive wouldn't be quite as peaceful. Something they never told you was how your entire life took a back seat to the nap schedule, after you'd had a child, but it was just as well they didn't tell you, because you would never have believed it, anyway.

One of the items-to-organize was the unfortunate fact she'd left her laptop at work, and even though she didn't have a lot of work assignments, just now, she should at least have it with her, even if it was nothing more than a prop to make her feel like she wasn't a complete dosser. To this end, she'd asked Munoz if she would drop it off whilst the other detective was out and about, doing her field work.

Doyle was packing her clothes when she received a text from Munoz, and hurried downstairs so that the other girl wouldn't have to hunt for a parking place. As the unmarked vehicle's passenger window was lowered, however, Doyle was met with a unexpected wave of hostility from an unhappy Munoz.

"Well, I just had a fun phone call, thanks to you. Whatever possessed you to tell Gabriel that I was in some sort of trouble?"

Doyle closed her eyes in chagrin. "Faith, I'm so sorry."

"He wanted to see if he could offer any help, and he wasn't inclined to believe me when I told him I wasn't in trouble, and that you were wrong."

Doyle decided that the best defense was to go on offense, and so she knit her brow in deep suspicion. "If you're truly not in trouble, then why did you meet with Acton? Never say you're gettin' promoted, instead?"

The other girl made a sound of derision. "Not on the heels of my DOD, idiot."

"Oh," Doyle realized. "Sorry. Faith, it's been a bad year, all 'round."

"Well, I got married, which pretty much makes the year a winner, in my book. I have some snaps from Dublin in my phone, if you'd like to see them."

But Doyle could recognize a diversion technique when she heard it, and narrowed her eyes suspiciously. "I think you're avoidin' my question, Munoz. Why were you meetin' with Acton?"

There as a long pause, whilst the other girl regarded her thoughtfully. "You may not want to hear it."

With some surprise, Doyle raised her brows. "What's this? Never say you were talkin' about *me*?"

She'd raised her voice, and so the parking valet turned his startled gaze to them. Both girls gave him a bright smile, and then Munoz stepped out of the vehicle and tossed him the keys. "We'll take a walk, but then we'll be right back."

"Yes, miss," said the valet, touching his hat, even though he was not supposed to allow an unattended vehicle out front. Munoz could trigger the man-switch at the drop of a hat, after all, and she wielded this superpower ruthlessly, when the occasion warranted.

The two detectives walked away on the pavement, and as soon as they were out of earshot, Doyle insisted, "You will tell me what's afoot, Munoz—I'm countin' to ten."

Munoz revealed in an even tone, "I met with Acton because I wanted to tell him about your hand—about how you favored it, sometimes."

"Oh," said Doyle, a bit deflated. This, of course, made sense, and she shouldn't have flown off the handle that way she had. "I see."

"I didn't tell anyone else, but I thought it was important to tell him."

Doyle nodded in understanding. "Well, you needn't have worried, Munoz; I was tryin' to hide it from him, but he already knew."

"No, he didn't know."

Turning her head to face the other girl, Doyle explained, "He may have pretended that he didn't already know, but Acton notices everythin'. I appreciate that you tried to keep it on the down-low, though."

Munoz was silent for a few steps, until she said, "No, he really didn't know. And I also thought it was important to tell him that sometimes you'd forget which hand was injured."

Doyle came to an abrupt halt, to stare at the other girl in abject astonishment. "*What?*"

Munoz came to a halt also, and turned to face her. "I

thought it might have been a symptom of post-traumatic stress syndrome, and so I decided it was best to go speak with Acton." She paused. "He told me you'd never favored it, in his presence. He had no idea."

As this recitation was true—every word—Doyle could only continue to stare in profound amazement. "Holy *Mother*," she breathed, as she slowly held up her hand to regard it. "I've run mad."

"Acton thought you may have wanted me to notice that something was wrong, so he suggested that I broach it with you."

"And you did," Doyle acknowledged, flexing her hand into a fist, and then spreading it open again. "And—I have to say—it's been better, ever since; I've been better, and more able to think straight. Faith, it's hard to believe I was bein' such a baby, cryin' out for attention."

Munoz shrugged. "You had an altercation with a suspect. It's textbook trauma, and a lot of coppers have lingering symptoms. I wondered if maybe you should go see the people in Counseling, but Acton thought we'd wait and see, since your symptoms were relatively mild."

Of course, Acton would want to wait-and-see, Doyle thought; because the last needful thing was to get the man's wife talking to a psychologist about what made her tick—or what made her husband tick, for that matter. Those were some still waters that ran a bit too deep, for your average government-employed shrink.

Oh, she thought, suddenly struck; and now I know why Dr. Harding showed up. Small wonder, that I couldn't figure out why he was the designated ghost, or why he didn't seem to have much to say except "very good." Think on it; I have friends—good friends, who are willing to intrude, and who will stand bluff—thank God fastin'—even though some of them may no longer be alive.

Blinking back tears, she offered in a halting voice, "Thank you, Izzy—I'm that grateful to you."

"Don't expect me to hug you," the other girl warned in alarm.

Her tone made Doyle laugh, and the emotional moment passed. "Faith, no; instead, I needed a good scoldin' to set me to rights, and you gave it to me, just like you're supposed to do—good works, during the holy season. Which only reminds me that I have to figure out some way to speak with Martina Betancourt; she needs a good scoldin', too."

Munoz narrowed her eyes. "Martina's at Wexton, and probably in the psych ward."

With all confidence, Doyle replied, "I'll get through to her; Wexton Prison owes me one."

Quickly, Munoz turned to begin the walk back to the building's entrance. "I'm going to pretend I didn't hear that. If you jeopardize the Crown's case on a murder-one, you'll be in worse trouble than I was with my DOD."

"Of course," Doyle soothed, as she hurried alongside her. "Forget I mentioned it, Munoz. And a scoldin' would probably do no good, in any event—Martina holds a grudge like no other."

"She'd only think that she had 'just cause' for her grudges," Munoz replied with a full measure of irony. "It must be very handy, to have 'just cause' to kill everyone who crosses you."

But Doyle corrected, "She didn't hold a grudge against her husband; she killed him out of kindness."

"Pull the other one," said Munoz, as the building loomed before them.

Shrugging in acknowledgment, Doyle admitted. "I suppose you've the right of it. And she definitely didn't kill Dr. James or the office manager out of kindness—both of those scenes were downright nasty." Frowning, she paused. "Why isn't Martina a suspect in the charge-nurse case? That was a nasty scene, too—not to mention that he was killed with a sword, and Martina wears that sword-necklace of hers, all the time."

With a show of extreme patience, Munoz replied, "No, Doyle; Martina can't be a suspect because the timeline doesn't add up. And besides, you have to be pretty strong to run a sword through a grown man's ribcage."

Acknowledging this basic truth, Doyle nodded in concession. "Right. It wasn't just any sword, either—some sort of collectible, Gabriel said."

"Not interested in what Gabriel has to say, Doyle."

But Doyle wasn't listening, because she was getting a signal that this was important, for some reason—but why? Gabriel had said the sword was a collectible, but they couldn't trace it, so that little factor didn't matter much, in terms of solving the case. Or—or mayhap he hadn't said it was a *collectible*, exactly; instead he'd said—he'd said that Sir Vikili had an ancient weapons collection.

Startled, she paused before the building's revolving doors, and briefly shut her eyes. Mother a' Mercy—could it be? Gabriel had hinted that there were some rumors going around about Sir Vikili—

"I'll be going," said Munoz, eyeing her. "Are you all right?"

"Oh—oh, yes—I'm fine, Munoz. I need the laptop, though."

"Oh—right; let me go fetch it."

Doyle found that she had to lean back against the building's wall, as she watched Munoz retrieve her keys from the smitten valet, and wondered—with no small horror—if it was remotely possible that the great Sir Vikili was going about murdering people with his stupid sword collection. It was a ridiculous notion—wasn't it? Why would such a man plot to kill the charge-nurse, in the first place? Of course, the charge-nurse had grassed-out his wretched brother, along with all the other blacklegs in the illegal pharmaceuticals rig. Come to think of it, if the famous solicitor was the type to have an ancient-weapons collection in the first place, mayhap he was also the type to hold blood-grudges against grassers.

But wait—wait a blessed moment; she was forgetting something—something important. Savoie was the one who'd stolen the sword from the pawn shop—this was a what you'd call a 'known-known,' and it didn't fit-in with the Sir Vikili-as-murderer theory. Unless, of course, the burglary was staged to erase the evidence trail back to Sir Vikili, and his collection. It wouldn't be the first time a burglary was staged so as to break the chain of evidence.

But try as she might, Doyle couldn't buy into this theory either, mainly because it seemed very unlikely that Savoie would perform such a favor for Sir Vikili. After all, Savoie had been betrayed by Sir Vikili, back when the solicitor had tried to frame him for murder, and Savoie was not exactly what you'd call the forgive-and-forget type. Neither was Acton, for that matter; faith, when she'd said to Munoz that Martina held a grudge like no other, she should have clarified that Acton was the undisputed champion of holding a grudge, and that Martina couldn't hold a candle—

Oh, she thought, nearly swaying with deep dismay; oh —how could I have missed this?

Munoz handed her the laptop, but since Doyle was having trouble concentrating over the roaring sound in her ears, it promptly slipped through her fingers and dropped to the pavement with a clatter.

As both girls immediately stooped to retrieve the broken laptop, Doyle chided herself grimly, lace up your boots, lass —you're back in the game with a vengeance.

CHAPTER 39

"Sorry, Munoz," Doyle said as they stood again, with Doyle cradling the broken laptop. "It's my fake-wonky hand."

"It's all right, Doyle," the other girl replied in a rare show of kindness. "I should have been more careful. Do you think it still works?"

"It doesn't matter; I can always borrow Acton's." Doyle mustered up a smile. "If I don't see you before, have a Happy Christmas—Geary, too."

"Thanks; you too." And with a final little wave to the valet who'd leapt to hold her car door, Munoz drove away.

Doyle, on the other hand, was thinking furiously—or as furiously as she was able—and trying to decide what was best to do. That Greek fellow's sword had been dangling right before her face the whole blessed time, and she'd been truly walking about in a fog not to have seen it before now. The reason she hadn't been able to shake the feeling that the charge-nurse's murder was somehow connected to the office manager's murder was because it was, and the connection was Doyle's rampaging husband, whose wife had run mad, and who was out for vengeance with a vengeance.

Savoie hadn't stolen the sword for Sir Vikili, he'd stolen it for Acton—the same time he'd stolen Acton's necklace, which was a huge clue, and if her brain had been working properly, she'd have realized the strangeness of it. Because if Acton wanted the necklace back, he'd have simply sent Trenton or someone in to claim it—the pawn shop thought it was a fake, after all. But instead he wanted a burglary—a burglary that also filched a murder weapon, which was a bushel more significant than some stupid old necklace.

And—as she'd realized all over again—Acton held a grudge like no other, which was part-and-parcel of the troubling fact that he tended to kill people who'd done her wrong. He'd been better, recently, but that particular Acton-leopard was not going to change his spots by lying down docilely when his home had been invaded, and the fair Doyle had barely managed to survive a life-and-death struggle on the stairway. He would crave vengeance, would Acton, and so he'd be doing what he did best: drinking deep, and executing his revenge.

But his murderous impulses would have been necessarily thwarted somewhat; Martina's wretched husband was already dead, and the evil Mr, Javid was likewise dead. Therefore, Acton would have to drop down to second-tier vengeance-victims, and the next two in line were Martina—who was responsible for their entry into the flat—and Sir Vikili, who'd managed to get his horrid brother out on his own recognizance so that he was free to go forth and wreak havoc on the fair Doyle.

Acton had framed Martina for the office manager's

murder, and he was in the process of framing Sir Vikili for the charge nurse's murder—that must be the "delicate matter" that Acton was discussing with the Crown Commissioner; their top solicitor was about to be charged with a sensational murder. It was ruthless retribution, Acton-style, and the fact that Munoz had told him that his poor wife was showing signs of an unsound-mind only fed his terrible resolve to make them pay, and pay dearly—forgiveness was never something in the Acton-equation.

A bit overwhelmed, Doyle paused as she walked slowly through her building's lobby. What could she do? Martina was locked away, and she'd the sense that Sir Vikili would be arrested at any moment, judging by Acton's outsized desire to bundle her out of town. She should try to stop it, but— short of turning-in her husband for multiple murders—how?

I'm stymied, she thought in frustration; what's to do?

Lifting her head, she was suddenly reminded that this was exactly what Dr. Harding had said—that she was stymied. She was stymied, because she couldn't just go speak to Martina, to ask if she'd killed the office manager, and hear the truth. And this, no doubt, was exactly the reason that the murder was staged as an unsound-mind; Martina wouldn't be out on bail or even held in ordinary Detention—instead, she'd be locked up tight where the fair Doyle couldn't get to her, under any circumstances.

Making a decision, Doyle turned toward the concierge's desk, and approached him with a friendly smile. "May I borrow your phone, please?"

"Certainly, ma'am." The fellow placed the phone set on the counter, and before he discreetly withdrew, she advised, "My laptop and my mobile are going to be repaired; d'you mind if I leave them here, for pick-up?"

"Certainly," the man repeated, and dutifully accepted Doyle's electronics.

Lifting the receiver, she dialed a number, and then waited for the pick-up. Say what you will, she thought; I'm not one to be stymied. I'd forgot, in all the fogginess.

CHAPTER 40

*A*fter Doyle was patched-through by the Met's operator, Officer Gabriel picked up on the other end of the line. "Gabriel, here."

"Ho, Gabriel—it's Doyle. I need you to drive me to Wexton Prison, if you don't mind. I'd ask Savoie, but he's worn out his welcome there, and Munoz is bein' all 'follow-the-rules', and such. She can't afford another DOD."

There was a small pause. "And I can?"

"You're a wily boyo; you'll come about."

"Is this another land mine?"

"Mayhap. Gird your loins."

"All right; I'll be there in ten minutes, loins girded."

Good; she needed someone to ferry her over to Wexton quick-like, but she also needed to sound-out Gabriel; she'd the uneasy feeling that he knew what Acton was about, and had brought up the sword-collection subject to probe how much she knew.

Doyle then called Tim McGonigal's office manager to ask

for Dr. Okafor's number, so as to ring the woman up. "Dr. Okafor; I've a massive favor to ask."

"Officer Doyle," the Nigerian woman said with great pleasure. "I will gladly do any favor you ask."

The fruit of good works, thought Doyle; I saved the day for her, once, and there's nothing to stop me from saving the day, yet again.

Very much heartened, she explained, "It's to do with the Prison Ministry, and it's a bit of a dicey situation. One of my friends is being held in Wexton, and I'd like to go pray with her. Since I'm a police officer they may frown on it, though, so I'm hopin' to be your assistant, instead, and fly under the radar. They won't mind at all if you ask to visit with her."

"Of course. When would you like to visit?"

"Well, now—if that's possible; I hope you can spare a half-hour or so." Doyle paused. "I think she's in urgent need of prayer."

"Well—yes, I can arrange for it. Tell me her name."

Doyle did so, and then cautioned, "Remember, don't mention me."

"I understand, Officer Doyle."

Doyle rang off, trying to decide if she should call Reynolds with a tale that would explain why she'd be not returning for a couple of hours—especially since she was supposed to be leaving for Trestles, as soon as Edward woke. Since this seemed beyond her powers, she instead said to the concierge, "I'm off on a secret errand to pick up a Christmas present. Cover for me, if anyone notices I'm gone."

The man smiled. "I will, ma'am."

Therefore, when Doyle spotted Gabriel pulling up in front, she made sure to wave to the concierge in a conspiratorial way, and then hurried out.

As she settled into the passenger seat, she began without preamble, "Tell me, Gabriel; how many minutes did you wait before runnin' to Munoz to grass on me? Less than ten?"

The young man grimaced slightly, as he pulled back into traffic. "I'm sorry. I wanted to offer my help, if it was needed."

"It wasn't. She wasn't in any trouble a'tall—she met with Acton about somethin' entirely innocutous—or whatever the word is—and let this be a lesson to me not to gossip like an archwife." Nothin' for it, she thought, and took a deep breath. "You seem to do a lot of gossipin', yourself, Gabriel. The pawn shop clerk comes to mind, not to mention you've a new girlfriend in Crown Court Liaison Services—you must hear a lot of chatter, from her."

He glanced over at her thoughtfully, and she'd the feeling that he knew exactly what she was getting at. "It pays to keep an ear to the ground."

"Well," she said carefully, "you may have heard some things that aren't true."

He considered this for a moment. "Things having to do with my gene pool?"

She blew out the breath she'd been holding. "Aye. I think it's all a big misunderstandin', and it will be straightened out very soon."

"Why are we going to Wexton?"

Leave it to Gabriel to put two and two together. "I'm afraid I'd rather not say," she admitted. "Sorry; it's not that I don't trust you, it's that I'm tryin' to straighten everythin' out, with as little fallout as possible." This of course, was not exactly true; Doyle wasn't at all certain that Gabriel could be trusted, especially if he'd figured out what Acton was up to.

But her companion apparently understood her concerns,

and was willing to address them. "No problem, Sergeant; I will be happy to aid and abet you," he replied easily. "Mainly because my bad year would have been many times worse, if it weren't for your husband. Tell me this, at least; am I going to be involved in a shoot-out, like the last time you went to Wexton?"

She smiled. "I'll make no promises. Stay sharp."

They drove for a few minutes in silence, until Doyle decided she should try to make friendly conversation in the hopes that her driver wasn't going to bring down ruin on the House of Acton. "Any leads on the Lady Abby case?"

"None. Howard was not involved, it seems, because we came up with the 'related vehicle' plates for the strolling couples, and everything checks out."

"Ach; that case is goin' as cold as a collier's well—unless someone comes forward with somethin'," Doyle acknowledged. "Will you file it as a Class A or a Class B?"

He glanced over at her. "Neither; it's not officially a cold case, because a homicide file was never opened."

"Oh—that's right. Acton said the evidence wasn't strong enough to pull it out of 'misadventure.'"

Gabriel nodded. "I agree with him. The medical evidence was equivocal, and if it was a homicide, the killer would have done a better job of covering his tracks, rather than leaving her where we found her."

He spoke the truth, and it certainly seemed as though they were unlikely to find out what, exactly, had happened. "Poor woman," said Doyle.

He shrugged slightly. "Perhaps not so 'poor' as an unsound-mind."

But Doyle insisted, "I do feel sorry for her, Gabriel; she'd an unsound-mind due to thwarted-love, and it sent her over the edge."

"I resent that, Sergeant; I'm the poster-child for thwarted-love, and you don't see me murdering anyone."

"Yet," Doyle teased.

He laughed, and then said, "A fair point. To prevent such an occurrence, help me to find a better path. Tell be about Nazy, for instance."

Doyle lifted her brows. "What about your girlfriend over at Crown Liaison Services?"

He shrugged. "She's not interesting enough, I'm afraid. I would like a bit more depth, so to speak."

Since the last needful thing was to have Gabriel wheedling Nazy for information, Doyle replied, "Faith, Gabriel; your gene pool is only half-Persian in the first place, so you shouldn't be so particular about such things. Go find yourself some nice girl who is clever enough to stand up to you, and your many deep depths."

He shrugged. "Munoz got married."

Doyle blew out an exasperated breath. "She's not the only fish in the clever-sea, Gabriel. I know it's hard, but you've no choice, now, and may as well get on with it. It would keep your mind busy—although not too busy," she cautioned. "If your mind's too busy, it drives you barkin' mad."

"Excellent advice," he said, and—as they were fast-approaching the prison—he asked, "What's the protocol?"

Ironically enough, Doyle did have a protocol, dating back from that long-ago time when she'd flown under the radar to visit a different prisoner. Trying not to think about how that little episode had gone all wrong, she directed, "There's a bus stop about a quarter-mile from the gate, and it you will park there and wait for me, I'd appreciate it."

"Certainly," he said, and it wasn't true.

"You shouldn't try to come in," she cautioned. "I've a cover-story for me, but it wouldn't fit you at all."

He glanced at her as they turned into the entry road to the prison. "This is sounding more and more like a shootout. I can almost hear the piano-player pause, while everyone in the saloon steps back a step."

Smiling, she shook her head. "It's not goin' to be a shoot-out, Gabriel—faith, I don't even have a gun with me. Instead I'm doin' good works—'tis the holy season, after all."

"If you say so," he replied, with a full measure of skepticism.

CHAPTER 41

*Y*et again, Doyle entered the grim recesses of Wexton Prison, and tried not to think about her prior visits to the place, or how the general atmosphere here was very hard for her to bear, being as everyone, down to the guards, was to some degree miserable.

I've got to stop being such a baby—I'm 'comforting the afflicted,' she scolded herself. Or 'visiting the imprisoned'—or both, I suppose. 'Admonishing the sinner' has flown right out the window, since this particular sinner is not, in fact, guilty of the sin I thought she was.

Dr. Okafor was waiting for her at the security check-in point, and smiled broadly when she saw Doyle, the colorful scarf that was twisted atop her head incongruous in the monotone, stark setting. "Hello, Kathleen.'"

Mentally crossing her fingers, Doyle showed the guard her personal ID as opposed to her police ID, and hoped the man wouldn't recognize the semi-famous Officer Doyle—

prison guards were from a different branch of law enforcement, and tended to have their own heroes.

No such luck, however; she'd forgot that she was something of a prison-guard-hero, too. "Officer Doyle," the man said with a smile. "It is good to have you back." With an arch look, he cautioned, "Stay off the rooftop."

"I will," she agreed, and hoped he'd keep his lip buttoned. "I'm only visitin' today as part of the Prison Ministry."

"Come, come," Dr. Okafor interrupted in a brisk voice. "We have only a limited time."

The man reviewed Dr. Okafor's paperwork, and frowned slightly. "We'll have to include a monitor for this one—she's in psych."

"Whatever is necessary," Dr. Okafor calmly replied. "The prisoner has dire need of our prayers."

So will I, when Acton finds out about this, thought Doyle, as they were escorted into the psych wing. Truth to tell, she hadn't thought much further than her urgent desire to get to Martina, but this one was going to be quite the challenge, for the illustrious Chief Inspector, when he discovered that his madwoman of a wife was visiting the prisoner he'd tucked away so efficiently. Ah well; one crisis at a time.

They entered the visitor's room—a grim, bare-bones affair —to await Martina's appearance on the other side of the glass panel. Tamping down a surge of anxiety, Doyle took a deep breath, as she sat in the chair, and wondered why no one ever thought to paint such places in a bright, cheerful color. Probably because there was no point, of course; the walls practically emanated equal parts bleakness and despair.

Dr. Okafor didn't seem much-affected, but she'd no doubt become accustomed to bleakness-and-despair, since she now worked in this wretched, wretched place, which—come to think of it—was only a small step better than the wretched free clinic, where evil people were thick on the ground, committing their evil deeds.

The doctor leaned over to ask Doyle in her soft voice, "This prisoner is Christian?"

Doyle considered her answer. "For some value of Christian, I suppose. You might say she's a headstrong sort of Christian."

"All are welcome in the vineyard," the other woman said placidly. "Would you like me to lead the prayers, or will you?"

Suddenly, Doyle realized yet another problem that she hadn't thought through; the stupid prison was awash in surveillance—a hard lesson you'd think she'd have learned, by now. She couldn't very well start talking to Martina about Acton's attempt to frame her, which only showed you that she hadn't planned this out very well. Faith; it was a shame that Martina didn't speak Gaelic, or that Doyle didn't speak Spanish—although anything said could be translated, so there seemed little point. What was she to do? Of all the dim-witted things she'd done, this seemed the most dim-witted of all—

Suddenly struck, she paused, and—with a mighty effort—pulled herself together. We do speak a common language, she realized; the most common language of all. Turning to Dr. Okafor, she replied, "I will lead, if you don't mind. It's rather a situation like Rebekah, in the tent."

There was a pause, whilst Doyle could see Dr. Okafor thinking over the implications raised by the Bible story about a scheming woman who tended to eavesdrop on other conversations.

The door to the prisoner's side opened with a clang, and

Martina was escorted in. Mentally, Doyle winced at the young woman's appearance; she was pale, and composed—like a saint, going to the stake. She seemed focused within herself, with little interest in worldly goings-on, anymore, and the only sign of life she showed was when her listless gaze rested upon Doyle. She paused in surprise, until the guard prodded her into the chair.

For her own part, Doyle had to fight an almost overwhelming urge to run for the door. The last time she'd seen Martina, she'd been bleeding on Edward's nursery floor, and so she had to shut her eyes briefly, so as to erase that image. Don't think about it, she instructed herself firmly. You've a job to do, and best get on with it.

Opening her eyes, Doyle said with as much confidence as she could muster, "Hallo Martina; this is Dr. Okafor, and we are visitin' from the Prison Ministry."

Martina raised her brows, and looked between her two visitors. "I'd rather see a priest, if you don't mind."

There was a hint of rebuke in the words, because the Prison Ministry was evangelical in nature, and Martina was the sort to think that evangelicals were heretics of the first order.

Hurriedly, Doyle explained, "You see, I'd like to talk about Susanna and the Elders. I think that situation may apply, here, and we only need a Daniel."

There was a slight pause. Susanna had been falsely accused, and Daniel—who'd shown remarkable interrogation skills, for someone in ancient times—had proved she was innocent.

But—with a serene expression—Martina only shook her head. "I've no need of a Daniel, Kathleen, Instead, I will wear a martyr's crown; I will walk thorough fire, and not be burned."

There was a small silence. Nonplussed, Doyle stared at the young woman, because she hadn't considered the possibility that Martina wouldn't want to be rescued, in the first place. It did make sense, though; she seemed—she seemed *fatalistic*, if that was the right word—a world-weary martyr, headed for the stake. Thwarted-love in ruins all around her, and nothing left to live for.

Whilst Doyle's heart sank, Dr. Okafor interrupted her thoughts. "Who is Susanna?" she asked in her soft voice.

Doyle blinked in surprise, but Martina explained in a kindly tone, "An Old Testament story. Your people would consider it apocryphal."

Doyle looked between both of them. "I haven't a *clue* what that means."

"The evangelicals do not believe the story of Susanna is true scripture," Martina replied, and could not hide a hint of pity.

"Oh—oh; right," said Doyle hurriedly, not wanting to get into a religious war, just now. "Not everyone agrees on everythin'." Pausing, she tried to think of another Bible character who was falsely accused—come on, Doyle, there were *heaps* of them. "How about instead, we talk about Joseph and Potiferous."

"Potiphar," both women corrected her in unison, and then they glanced at each other in amusement, at having done so.

Good—good; a small sign of life, thought Doyle. "Yes, well; whatever his name was, it is important that the wicked not prosper. You can't just give up, and stop fightin' for justice."

But Martina continued unmoved. "I have finished the

race, Kathleen. I will wear a martyr's crown, and lie beneath the Fifth Seal, along with the souls of those who have been slain, for the witness they bore. I am reconciled; *if anyone suffers as a Christian, let him not be ashamed."*

Hearing the grim determination that underpinned these words, Doyle again closed her eyes briefly, struggling to come up with a rejoinder. "Please, Martina—"

But her words were interrupted by Dr. Okafor, who offered in a stern tone, "But surely, *a false witness should not go unpunished, nor should a liar escape."*

Like a dog who was hearing a distant horn, Martina slowly turned her gaze to meet the African woman's.

Dr. Okafor nodded gravely. *"You shall not spread a false report. You shall not join hands with a wicked man to be a malicious witness."*

Martina drew her brows together. "But—but I am not the one bearing false witness; I am not a sinner."

Dr. Okafor 's soft voice rose in reprimand, and the imperative words resonated off the walls in the small, dingy room. *"You shall confute every tongue that rises against you in judgement; this is the heritage of the servants of the Lord."*

Seeing her opening, Doyle added, "We're called to admonish the sinner, Martina—not to let 'im sin away, and thus lose any hope of salvation. It's all part of the Works of Mercy—seven, or eight, or however many—I forget."

Solemnly, Dr. Okafor nodded. *"You must put on the full armor of God,"* she declared in rolling tones, *"and those that revile you must be put to shame."*

Slowly, Martina offered, "Yes—I hadn't considered that aspect, of course."

"And you can't just plead guilty, and try to bootstrap

yourself under the Fifth Seal, with all the martyrs," Doyle added. "I don't think it works that way."

"No." Martina frowned, as she lowered her gaze to the linoleum desk before her. "It was my own pride, to think so. My pride has been my stumbling block."

"Well, you've an unsound-mind, too," Doyle noted fairly.

Their conversation was interrupted, however, when the monitor's phone pinged, and the outer guard's face appeared in the reinforced window with an expression a guard would have when he was worried that there was trouble brewing. When the heavy door swung open, Doyle was not at all surprised to behold Acton, standing between the guard and the Women's Warden.

There was a small silence, and Doyle swallowed. "Hallo, Michael."

Before Acton could reply, Martina rose to her feet. "I did not kill the woman you believe I did. I demand new counsel, and I wish to retract my plea."

"Certainly," said Acton.

CHAPTER 42

*D*oyle rose, and made the introductions. "You remember Dr. Okafor, Michael—she was our clinic witness. Well, not the only one—the charge-nurse too, of course, but he's now dead—"

"I do," interrupted Acton, who took the doctor's hand. "It is nice to see you again, doctor."

The Warden was understandably confused. "I'm terribly sorry, Chief Inspector Acton; I was informed this was a Ministry visit."

"It is," Doyle assured the woman. "Believe me, everyone's gettin' themselves admonished, left and right."

"I see," the woman replied, even though it seemed clear she didn't. With an attitude of apology, she leaned in to say, "I'm afraid I must be careful about what I allow and don't allow, because there have been complaints that the Ministry is taking over the prison."

"Well, we can't have that," Doyle said, and carefully refrained from meeting Dr. Okafor's eye.

"New evidence has come to light concerning this prisoner's case," Acton offered smoothly. "And a rescission of her plea is in the works."

He refrained from mentioning that this would come as a great surprise to the Crown Prosecutors, but Doyle followed his lead nonetheless. "Aye; she'd originally pled guilty out of guilt, I think, and now it's all been straightened out."

"I'm glad to hear it; all's well that ends well," the Warden agreed generously. "If you'd like to come to my office, Chief Inspector, I can call for coffee." After a slight pause, she continued, "Perhaps I could take a snap, with the two of you?"

Doyle smiled, because the no-nonsense woman seemed the last person you'd imagine to be a fan, but on the other hand, she'd long-ago noticed that any bureaucrat worth their salt loved to hang accolades on the wall.

"Of course," said Doyle, hoping that Acton wouldn't countermand the coffee, considering the situation.

But she'd underestimated her husband's raging desire to bundle her into the car, and so he was firm to the point of brusqueness. "We must be leaving, I'm afraid."

"I'd like to visit the roof, first," said Doyle in a bright tone. "I've fond memories of the roof." She met her husband's gaze with a message.

In some surprise, the Warden ventured, "It's rather cold, up there, this time of year."

"Just for a minute," Doyle wheedled. "For old time's sake."

"Certainly," her husband agreed after just the barest hesitation.

He thinks I've run mad, she decided, as they bade farewell to Dr. Okafor, and dutifully posed for a snap with the Warden. And small blame to the man for thinking it, but Dr. Okafor has lit an admonishing fire under me—and isn't it just like the evangelicals to do so, being as my own tribe tends to startle easily, and scuttle away.

And so, the guard escorted them to the stairwell, where they clanged up the narrow metal stairs to the roof access, the sound echoing in the small space, and Doyle making a mighty effort to fight the memories it provoked.

The guard turned off the emergency alarm, and once again, Doyle stepped out onto the roof of Wexton Prison, only this time it was empty, and a bit bleak, with only the occasional vent rising up to break the monotonous grey roofing tiles.

It was indeed cold, with threatening clouds overhead, and so she crossed her arms tightly—being as she wasn't wearing a coat—and immediately Acton shrugged out of his suit jacket, and placed it around her shoulders. As he drew the jacket close around her, he bent to peer into the eyes. "Are you all right, Kathleen?"

She offered-up a wan smile. "Well, there's no bridge to jump off, so this will have to do. I wanted to remind myself that I'm not so very helpless—that I've been brave before, and no doubt I'll be brave again."

He enfolded her in his arms, and rested his chin on her head. "You are the bravest person I know."

She smiled into his shirtfront, because it was the truth. "Well, you think you're strong and brave, until the moment that you're not, and here's hopin' I'm not bringin' on another round of PSTD, or whatever it's called."

Gently, he remonstrated, "You mustn't forget that you are pregnant, Kathleen."

She nodded, and rested her forehead against his chest. "I

do forget—it's the strangest thing. With the first one, it's all you think about, and with the second, you forget for days at a time—it's such old hat."

"Yes, but it does complicate matters. Shall I speak to McGonigal about whether there are appropriate medications you could take, to help you recover? He'd be discreet."

She leaned her head back to look up at him. "I don't think it's needful, Michael—my hand on my heart. I'm makin' amazin' progress—faith, you should have seen me leap into action, today."

He drew her to him again, and she could hear the thread of amusement in his voice. "I was astonished, indeed."

"Did Gabriel grass me out?"

"He did."

She blew out a breath. "I can't blame him, I suppose, but you've got to be careful, Michael. I think Gabriel knows a lot more than he's lettin' on, and he's not goin' to stand idly by whilst you ruin Sir Vikili—we've seen how powerful these tribal loyalties are."

Acton made no response, being as he'd probably been hoping she'd only caught wind of the send-Martina-to-prison plan, and not the additional send-Sir-Vikili-to prison-also plan. And now here she was, throwing yet another spanner into his wheel-of-vengeance-works; it must be frustrating beyond words, after having set it all up so carefully, and when sweet revenge was so close at hand.

Faith, I almost feel sorry for him—small wonder he's been drinking deep, she thought. And since it's mighty cold out here, and the man's trying not to shiver in his shirtsleeves, I'd best cut to the nub.

Squeezing his waist gently, she began, "I'm not going to give you my usual bear-garden jawin', Michael, because you've been doin' so well, lately—and don't think I haven't noticed. You were doin' much better, 'till the stupid donnybrook went down, and now you've backslid a bit. But let's dust ourselves off, and try to go forward again, instead of pullin' down the pillars around our heads." She paused, and then said with some significance, "I think Sir Vikili is wary, and knows what you're doin'—he's no fool."

"Of course, he does," Acton said quietly, over her head. "That is the entire point of the exercise, Kathleen."

His tone was clipped, and she could hear the barely-suppressed anger in his voice, and so she smoothed her hands across his chest in a soothing motion. "I know you've murder-in-the-blood, my friend, and that always seems the logical route, but it's a lot harder to forgive, than it is to go about killin' people to suit your fancy."

She could feel him draw breath, his chest rising and falling. "I'm afraid I can't be that generous, Kathleen."

"I'd like you to try, though. Think on it; if you bring down Sir Vikili, there'll be no one left to act as a check on you—save me, of course—and my plate is full enough."

He didn't respond, but bent his head to press his cheek against her temple, and tighten his grip around her—filled with remorse, he was, which was not altogether a bad thing, to try to bump him back from the ledge.

"Let him wriggle off the hook, Michael. Otherwise, I'll be forced to give him an alibi by claimin' I was in bed with him at the time o' death, which would be a hard sell, because there's not a soul alive who's goin' to believe that I'm a schemin' trollop."

"You don't dare," he countered, his voice resonating against the bones of her face. "You wouldn't bear false witness."

She paused in surprise. "Holy Mother; the devil is citin' scripture."

He chuckled, and she chuckled, but she sensed that he hadn't capitulated, and so she continued, "You need to fix this, Michael. Please—'tis the season of forgiveness."

Slowly, he replied, "I don't know as I can forgive them, Kathleen; they deserve every ounce of what is coming."

Leaning back, she met his eyes in all sincerity. "Deserve's got nothin' to do with it, Michael. That's the hardest thing to understand about forgiveness, I think—the hardest thing of all—but we're called to do it, anyways. D'you think it's easy for me to forgive them? They'd taken Edward, and they were goin' to—were goin' to—"

Suddenly, she bent her head, overcome, and fighting tears. She withdrew her arms from around him, and crossed them before her, tucking a hand under each arm.

Silently, he gathered her to him, and held her tightly as she sobbed, "It was *horrid*, Michael. He was so evil, and I'm glad he's dead, even though I shouldn't be." She wept uncontrollably for a few moments, her shoulders heaving until—wiggling a hand free—she wiped away her tears with a palm, and reminded herself that she wasn't helping matters, here; her husband didn't do well when she wept.

To this end, she took a fortifying breath, and tried to calm herself down. "It was horrid, and we're lucky Edward's not old enough to remember. He didn't even cry, Michael; he just looked at them the way he does when he's that annoyed with you."

"I know that look," Acton said.

She laughed, and he relaxed his hold on her, so as to retrieve his handkerchief, and offer it to her. "Would it help to do a walk-through, perhaps?"

A "walk-through" was when detectives retraced the events of the crime. "Faith, no," she declared, dabbing at her eyes. "Let's not call down that whirlwind." Not to mention she'd her very own top-shelf psychiatrist, on call.

With a gentle movement, he smoothed her hair away from her face. "Perhaps we should move, Kathleen."

She blew out a breath, and fiddled with a button on his shirtfront. "No," she decided. "But I'd appreciate it if you did lay carpet on the stairs—somethin' pretty, and colorful." She brushed the back of her hand against his shirt, thinking that some ash had fallen on it, until she realized that it had started snowing.

Leaning back, she looked up in surprise, and he did the same, as the soft flakes suddenly filled the air around them.

In a quiet voice, Doyle said, "Tell me you'll back down, husband."

"Yes," he said, and drew her to him again.

"For both of them," she clarified. One could never be too careful, when exacting promises from Acton.

"For both of them," he replied, and it was the truth.

Why, I believe he's relieved, she realized, as she clung to his waist, and the snow began falling in earnest. Mayhap he's not as bloody-minded as he pretends.

She added, "And there's one last thing; promise you'll stop sendin' people to Maghaberry Prison, so as to have them murdered."

He went still, and she could sense his profound surprise, as the snow continued to fall around them.

"Don't try to deny it," she advised; "there are various ghosts who are always willin' to grass you out."

"If I were you," he said slowly, "I'd say, 'Holy Mother'."

"As well you should." Since some of the flakes had caught

in her eyelashes, she rubbed her face, back and forth against his shirt. "I know that this was one of those 'multiple cause' situations, and so I can't blister you like an archwife, this time around. I'm truly sorry I gave you such a scare, Michael, and I'm truly sorry things happened the way they did, but you've got to try to control your murderous impulses. We had a close call, and let this be a lesson."

Suddenly struck, she lifted her face to his. "When you think about it, it's like that story—that Christmas-Magi story. We got into this mess because we know each other so well; I was tryin' to keep my hurts from you, because I knew what your reaction would be, and you were tryin' to keep your revenge-doings from me, because you knew what my reaction would be. And so, we made everythin' miles worse, which is exactly what happened in the story. I don't know why everyone thinks it's such a sweet story—they were crackin' idiots, between them."

"Perhaps," he agreed.

"No 'perhaps' about it," she declared. "A couple of mawkish knockers who deserved exactly what they got."

"Do you mind if we discuss this in the car?" he asked. "I am afraid that I can no longer feel my fingers."

She smiled, and lifted her face for his kiss. "Let's go in, then; I think everything's as wrapped up as it can be, considerin' it's you and it's me."

CHAPTER 43

They returned to the flat, so as to have a casual supper on the floor by the fire, with Reynolds expressing his discreet dismay at the state of the master's suit jacket, as he carried it away.

Acton then retreated to his office—no doubt to unravel some of the threads he'd been weaving—and as she lay before the warm fire, Doyle was not at all surprised to discover that she'd fallen asleep, after such a tumultuous day.

"Caught him out," she declared to Dr. Harding, as she stood on the rocky outcropping. "And not a moment too soon, I might add."

"A good day's work," he agreed.

"I'm glad you're here—I wanted to say thanks."

"It was my pleasure," he replied, as he regarded her over his spectacles. "And not completely unexpected, of course."

She sighed. "No; and I suppose you're goin' to tell me that I was hidin' under the bed, because I knew what was comin', and I didn't want to have to deal with it."

He nodded. "Very good," he said.

She smiled at him. "Not so 'very good' that it took me this long to shake my stumps; it's just like I told him—you think you're strong and brave, until the moment that you're not."

He tilted his head slightly. "There is courage in overcoming one's fear, certainly."

She sighed. "Aye. Well, I needed a bit o' help to do it, this time around. I never had many friends, growin' up—bein' as I am, and everythin'. But now I do have friends—friends who are willin' to intrude so as to straighten me out. It's a strange and unlooked-for happenstance, but there it is."

"Societal and group support," he agreed. "Often helpful in maintaining mental equilibrium; a by-product of the time when such support was needed for sheer survival." He paused, and then noted fairly, "Although there are cases where the instinct to build such support does more harm than good."

This remark hung in the air, and so Doyle ventured into the ensuing silence, "Are you talkin' about thwarted-love? Because there's been heaps of it, lately."

Dr. Harding cocked his head, considering this. "No; more along the lines of a nostalgia for feelings which have been extinguished. His mother died young, and she was a Madonna-like figure for him; he has now projected it onto a similar woman—a classic maternal transference."

At sea, Doyle stared at him. "Are we talkin' about Acton? Because Acton's mother's still very much alive, and she's the furthest thing from a Madonna-like figure you could possibly imagine."

With a small smile, the psychiatrist agreed, "Indeed. If his was a maternal transference, your husband wouldn't dote on you, certainly."

Doyle agreed, "Aye, that; instead there'd be scorched earth for miles, with no nostalgia anywhere to be found. All in all, it's just as well that we hardly see her, even though she's Edward's only gran."

The psychiatrist spread his hands. "Not at all. Happy Christmas, Ms. Doyle."

And then Doyle was standing before a familiar door, worn and battered, but bravely sporting a holly-bough, hanging on a nail. In wonder, she ran her hand over the door's rough surface, and then, after hesitating for a moment, pushed it open.

Inside, her mother bent by the oven in the cramped kitchen, checking on the contents which were baking within. She was young, and vibrant, and the dim room was lit up like no other room Doyle had been in, ever since.

With a smile, her mother glanced up at her. "There you are, Kathy; keep the cold out, please—there's a good lass."'

With an effort, Doyle found her voice. "Aye, mum," she whispered.

And then, in a blink, her mother was gone—back to the place where it never wasn't Christmas, and no one ever let the cold in.

$\mathcal{T}$he next morning, Doyle and Acton were in the car, starting out for Trestles with Edward sitting in his car seat behind them. It amused him no end to have his mother pretend to feed his dinosaur toy with his sipping-cup, and so she was performing this function whilst he watched and giggled.

"Never thought I'd be feeding a bottle to a dinosaur," she remarked. "It just goes to show."

"I never thought I'd be driving to Trestles with a wife, and a son," Acton replied.

"A son and a half," she corrected.

He smiled. "Just so."

"Life's a crackin' amazement," she observed. "If Father John were here, he'd speak of signs and wonders."

Her husband glanced at her. "He will have Christmas dinner with McGonigal, this year. I dropped a word about having a blood pudding, on the menu."

"Oh—oh, thank you for takin' care of him, Michael; I've

got to start gatherin' up the threads, and catchin' myself up with everythin'."

"You will rest," her husband said in a firm tone. "And that's an order."

She smiled. "Yes, sir."

Doyle continued to ply the sipping-cup, and glanced back to say to Edward, "He has a hollow leg, this fellow," which made her son laugh with delight. Idly, she looked up from the task for a moment, and watched as the snow hit the windscreen, in between being wiped away by the wipers. "My mother called me Kathy."

She could sense her husband's surprise, as he glanced over at her. "Did she? Would you like me to call you Kathy?"

She smiled. "Faith no; you're not my mother, Michael. I'm just feelin' nostalgic, I think—we'd make a ginger cake at Christmas, my mum and me. Sugar was very dear, but she saved up for it, because she was determined to have ginger cake at Christmas, and no sacrifice was too great. We'd bake it together, and it was the best thing I've ever tasted, before or since." She paused, watching the snow. "D'you think Reynolds can show me and Edward how to make a ginger cake?"

He reached to take her hand. "I will help, instead."

She laughed. "You've never baked anythin' in your life, Michael."

"I will bake ginger cake. How hard can it be?"

"Don't ask me. It will be the blind leadin' the blind."

They drove for a few more minutes, until they came to the gated parking lot that led into the Inns of Court. After Acton showed his ID to the guard, he pulled the car up next to the entry, and then bent to glance up at the building through the windscreen. "The weather's a little rough," he cautioned. "Perhaps this visit might be postponed?"

"It will take just a minute, Michael; but it's important." She paused. "It's a bit hard to explain."

He nodded, because he knew all there was to know about the things she found hard to explain. "Try not to say anything you shouldn't."

She smiled at him as she pulled on her coat. "It's me, Michael; that's my standard operatin' procedure." As she opened the door, she added, "If I'm not back in twenty minutes, send an extraction team."

Doyle made her way to the top floor of the prestigious building, and gave the receptionist her name, before settling in to wait in one of the posh leather chairs. The place was elegantly furnished, and not for the first time, Doyle thought, he's a lot like Acton—it's that alpha-lion thing, mayhap. They are very fond of their trophies, these alpha-lions.

Almost immediately, the great man himself appeared at his chambers door, doing only a fair job of hiding his extreme surprise. "Officer Doyle; please, come in."

As she sat in one of the client's chairs across from Sir Vikili's massive desk, Doyle couldn't help but think of the countless blacklegs who'd no doubt sat in the same chair, and surreptitiously stole a quick glance at the painting on the wall —a painting that showed a scene from an epic Persian love story.

I've my own epic love story, she thought, as she turned to face him; I should have Javid paint a scene from it, too, but there are so many to choose from it would hard to decide. Mayhap I should go with the most obvious one; two detectives on a stake-out, having the most awkward conversation in the history of awkward conversations.

It was clear that Sir Vikili was nonplussed, but he was not one to be at a loss for words, and so he began with all sincerity. "I must offer my profound apologies, Officer Doyle. I deeply regret the injuries my family has bestowed upon yours."

"Oh, I'm not here about that," Doyle assured him. "All's forgiven, even if it's not so very easy to forget." She pulled out a plain brown paper bag from her coat pocket. "I wanted to give you this—to return it." Carefully, she shook-out the sapphire necklace onto his desk.

There was a moment of silence, as he stared at the glittering jewels in profound surprise. "You—you wish to return this? Officer Doyle, please—please, I cannot accept. Let us agree it is a small price to pay for your troubles." He attempted a smile, and spread out his palms. "In truth, I believe it originally belonged to an English countess, and so it is only fitting."

"I never want to see the wretched thing again as long as I live," Doyle declared. "Either you take it, or it winds up in the pond at Trestles."

"I—I don't know what to say."

Doyle stood to leave. "I imagine you don't celebrate Christmas, and so instead, I'll give it to you as a weddin' present."

With some bewilderment, her companion also rose to his feet, and stared at her. "But—but Officer Doyle, I am not getting married."

Doyle smiled. "I think you are, sir, and I wish you every happiness."

CHAPTER 45

*W*hen Doyle returned to the car, it was to find that her husband was showing their son a compilation of nursery rhymes on his mobile, being as he was not the sort of person who was going to pretend to feed a dinosaur for love or money.

He glanced up at her as she settled into the car. "Everything all right?"

"Right as rain," she replied. "I broke off our affair, and he was very sorry to hear it."

"That is a shame. I can almost sympathize."

She laughed at this out-and-out lie. "Well, you shouldn't waste your pity—everything's turned up a trump for him, mainly because he's not molderin' away in a faraway Irish prison." She glanced at him sidelong, even though she knew there was little chance he'd tell her what he'd done to extract Sir Vikili from the spider's web he'd been weaving—her husband liked to play his cards very close to the vest. "Instead, he's now free to keep crossin' swords with you—

whilst stayin' all polite, and such—which is exactly how it should be."

"If you say," said Acton, which was an equivocal answer if she'd ever heard one.

"One-a-penny, two-a-penny," Edward sang, although if you didn't already know what he was saying, you'd have no clue.

As they pulled onto the main thoroughfare, she teased, "Will your piano at Trestles allow you to play nursery rhymes on it, or is it too fancy for the likes of nursery rhymes?"

But her husband's response was not what she'd expected, as he replied earnestly, "This visit, I thought I'd see if Edward will sit on my lap for a bit. I think he shows a musical aptitude."

"Clearly," Doyle agreed in a serious tone, and then hid a smile as the little boy warbled off-key.

He glanced over at her. "Shall we stop along the way, and let him play in the snow?"

"His mittens are packed somewhere, Michael."

"We can call Reynolds, to find out where."

"Let's wait for Trestles," she decided. "The boyo's not one for half-measures, and so he'll be soaked to the bone; best have a hot bath at the ready."

"A good point; I will be ready for one, myself."

With a great deal of meaning, she offered, "Mayhap I'll join you, husband, since the pond is probably too cold, this time o' year."

Acton smiled, and took her hand. "Now, there's a brilliant idea."

"Hot cross buns," sang Edward.

"Exactly," Doyle agreed.

EPILOGUE

A *shame, that the plan had not been successful, but no matter; he would be patient, and indeed, it was a difficult puzzle. In the end, it would be worth it, of course—she stood as a mother to his son, and his son deserved no less. A kind woman, and loving. Restful; it was time to have a restful woman at home, with no ambition other than to care for her family, and to pray at church —someone like his own chère mère, before she'd been taken from him, far too soon.*

So; perhaps more evidence could be made to surface, in the drowning case? Nothing too obvious, of course—it was a delicate balance. Quel dommage, that the bait had not been taken.

There could always be an accident, of course. Again, he'd have to be very careful that no trail would lead back to him. Emile would have a good mother, and a sister he already loved. As for him, he would have a good wife—a devoted wife, and he would buy her a large house; large enough to house them all, with a yard for the children to play. Many children, he decided; he liked children.

"Papa," his son called out. "Watch me!"
"Bien sûr," he called back, and smiled.

CPSIA information can be obtained
at www.ICGtesting.com
Printed in the USA
LVHW031403180521
687776LV00017B/203

9 781734 431643